A Wartime Secret

ANNIE MURRAY was born in Berkshire and read English at St John's College, Oxford. Her first 'Birmingham' story, *Birmingham Rose*, hit the *Sunday Times* bestseller list when it was published in 1995. She has subsequently written twenty-one full-length novels, including the best-selling ·*Chocolate Girls* and *War Babies*. Annie has four children and lives near Reading.

BY THE SAME AUTHOR

Birmingham Rose
Birmingham Friends
Birmingham Blitz
Orphan of Angel Street
Poppy Day
The Narrowboat Girl
Chocolate Girls
Water Gypsies
Miss Purdy's Class
Family of Women
Where Earth Meets Sky
The Bells of Bournville Green
A Hopscotch Summer
Soldier Girl
All the Days of Our Lives
My Daughter, My Mother
The Women of Lilac Street
Meet Me Under the Clock
War Babies
Now the War is Over

ANNIE MURRAY

A Wartime Secret

PAN BOOKS

First published 2017 by Pan Books
an imprint of Pan Macmillan
20 New Wharf Road, London N1 9RR
Associated companies throughout the world
www.panmacmillan.com

ISBN 978-1-5098-7002-8

Copyright © Annie Murray, 2017

The right of Annie Murray to be identified as the
author of this work has been asserted by her in accordance
with the Copyright, Designs and Patents Act 1988.

All rights reserved. No part of this publication may be reproduced,
stored in a retrieval system, or transmitted, in any form, or by any means
(electronic, mechanical, photocopying, recording or otherwise)
without the prior written permission of the publisher.

Pan Macmillan does not have any control over, or any responsibility for,
any author or third-party websites referred to in or on this book.

1 3 5 7 9 8 6 4 2

A CIP catalogue record for this book is available from the British Library.

Typeset in Stempel Gramond 11/13.2 pt by
Palimpsest Book Production Limited, Falkirk, Stirlingshire

Printed and bound by CPI Group (UK) Ltd, Croydon, CR0 4YY

This book is sold subject to the condition that it shall not, by way of
trade or otherwise, be lent, hired out, or otherwise circulated without
the publisher's prior consent in any form of binding or cover other than
that in which it is published and without a similar condition including
this condition being imposed on the subsequent purchaser.

Visit www.panmacmillan.com to read more about all our books
and to buy them. You will also find features, author interviews and
news of any author events, and you can sign up for e-newsletters
so that you're always first to hear about our new releases.

Foreword

This year WHSmith celebrates its 225th anniversary, and to mark this momentous occasion we are pledging to raise £2 million to split between three charities: Cancer Research UK, Mind and the National Literacy Trust.

Several authors have kindly agreed to supply WHSmith with exclusive short stories in order to enable us to offer customers something new to the market and to donate £1 from each sale, split equally between the chosen charities.

We do hope you enjoy reading these specially chosen titles, and join us in thanking the authors for their support.

Sandra Bradley
Trading Controller
Fiction Books

This story is not about the Land Girls, but special thanks go to Marjorie Eglinton of Shirley, Birmingham, who worked as a Land Girl and kindly told me many stories – including the one about the rabbit.

I

One

As soon as she saw the telegraph boy at her door with his bike in the pouring rain, she knew.

'Oh . . . Oh no!'

One hand flew to her chest, her pounding heart. Quickly she lowered it again, trying not to look like the madwoman she felt, in her apron, her unbrushed hair falling all over the place, still holding the baby's spoon coated in mashed potato.

She tried to take the telegram from him calmly. Shutting the door, she leaned against it, hearing the muffled chatter of the wireless from the back room. If it was bad news, weren't they supposed to ask you if you were on your own? Through all these years of war she had dreaded a telegram arriving like this . . .

Daring herself, she looked at the envelope in her hand. *Grace Chapman, 21 Inkerman Street . . .*

'Oh my God,' she whispered.

She managed to get back to the kitchen, her legs like water as she sank down at the table, hands shaking so much she could hardly open the envelope. She was oblivious to everything: to the rain falling outside, to little Barbara chuckling to herself where Grace had hurriedly laid her on a blanket on the linoleum.

HOME TONIGHT. SIX WEEKS LEAVE. TED.

She gasped, the words burning into her.

Getting unsteadily to her feet, she went to the battered sideboard and clicked off the wireless. In the sudden quiet she stared at the telegram lying on the faded pink flowers of the tablecloth: this message from the husband she had not seen for more than five years. A husband whose only communications had been the briefest of letters sent through by the Red Cross. And she had written back, trying to sound hopeful, trying to draw him close to her again, while feeling as if she was throwing stones out into the darkness. Here in front of her now were the words she had yearned to read for so long. She had heard no bad news of Ted, other than that he had been taken prisoner, back in 1940. Sooner or later, she had thought, he must come home. But now . . . The words terrified her; made her feel as if she was on trial.

What kind of wife are you, Grace Chapman?

Her daughter's gurglings returned her attention to the little back room in her two-up two-down terrace with its exhausted old furniture: the old sideboard, scullery with a sink, the black range with a grubby rag rug beside it and scrubbed deal table. On the table rested the bowl of mashed potato and gravy and on the blanket the baby with gravy-potato on her face and encrusted in her cap of fair hair . . .

'Oh, *Baba*!' Her little girl looked stricken for a second at her tone, then chortled happily, waving her plump feet in the air. Grace could not help a second's smile, even though she felt liquid with nerves. 'Look at the state of you! You'll have to have the rest of your dinner later, babby – we've got to go . . .'

So agitated she could not think straight, she scuttled

about the room, muttering out loud as she shoved bits and pieces for Barbara into a cloth bag. *What am I going to do? He's coming back. He's really coming – today, tonight. What can I say to him? Lord above – what do I do?*

'Come on, babby . . .' Frantic, she scooped Barbara up into her arms and rushed out of the house.

Two

Nothing about Inkerman Street was different from usual that afternoon: the rows of soot-stained terraced houses, a number of them smashed into bombsites; the pubs and factories; the entries leading to back yards. It was an unremarkable day, with a quiet flatness to things. The war was over – for Europe, in any case. The air felt close and muggy, smelling of recent rain, with the sun trying to break through. The coalman was delivering to a nearby house, children were turning skipping ropes on the cobbled street, mothers sat or stood in doorways in the shade . . . A normal day.

Yet to Grace in her frantic state, everything felt electrified with a sense of crisis. She knew she must look a state, her wavy black hair all over the place, stains down her pale-blue white-spotted dress, but none of that mattered. *Ted's coming home, he's coming today* played like a tattoo in her head.

She glanced back at her own little terraced house as she set off, at the faded blue door and tarnished knocker, the front windows shrouded by aged net curtains, and it appeared suddenly strange to her, as if she never usually looked at it. The air, the fall of the light – everything seemed different. *Ted. Home. Really coming back after all this time* . . . He had been away for longer than they had been married before he left. *Ted, my husband.* Her feet beat out the rhythm. *The man I love* . . . She was choked with emotion.

Ted, the man to whom she had faithfully written, trying to keep alive the love they had for each other on their wedding day, an eternity ago when she was twenty-two and he twenty-three. Ted, who even now was moving closer – was he on a train? – closer by the moment . . .

Holding Barbara tightly, the bag swinging on her arm, she walked as fast she could without breaking into a run. She didn't want to attract attention, but she just *had* to get there. She had her wits about her just enough to dodge the wettest patches of pavement, as there were holes in her shoes.

As she scurried along, it felt as if the Grace who had kissed Ted goodbye after his last leave in 1940, and she, the Grace of today, five years later, were trying to reunite, and they could barely recognize each other.

Who was I then? And who am I now?

She glanced down at her feet in the scuffed shoes, walking the blue-brick pavement. Even her feet seemed strange to her. She felt like crying for a moment, thinking of that time of innocence before the war.

Since then, too much had happened. *He* had happened. And *Barbara* had happened.

Barbara, this warm, blue-eyed, beautiful five-month-old weight in her arms. This child, gazing at the houses as if seeing everything for the first time and in whose wide, curious eyes, it was all good and right.

Grace hammered on the door of an attic-high terraced house two streets away and pushed the door open.

'Joan?' Her voice was a shriek as she rushed along the narrow hall.

'Here.' Her sister's voice came from the back. The house was crammed full of furniture and children and Norman's train sets and Joan's knitting.

Joan was sitting in her kitchen, barefoot in the warmth,

her youngest, Davey, playing with wooden bricks at her feet.

'He's coming back. Tonight!'

Joan gaped at Grace as she burst in, and pushed her heavy body up in the chair. For a moment Grace felt wild impatience with her sister for being plump and stolid, something for which she was normally grateful. Joan had been Grace's comfort all her life – rock-like, sensible, slow, while Grace was thin and wiry, her black hair tumbling wildly at every age. Even Joan's hair was calmer – jet black but straighter and more manageable. She wore it up in a loose bun.

'*Tonight?*'

'I've just had the telegram . . .'

Barbara was holding out her arms towards her cousin Davey. Grace laid her down next to him and plonked herself on the edge of the chair opposite her sister.

'What the hell'm I going to *do*, Joan?'

They were the same words she had used when she found out she was expecting Barbara. Back then, Joan had yelled at her, 'You're *what*? You stupid, *stupid* . . .' But now, Joan rolled her eyes and got wearily to her feet, pushing a strand of hair back into her bun.

'What d'you want me to say? Look, Grace, we've been over this no end of times. You've made your bed and you'll have to lie on it.' She plonked the kettle down on the gas and turned. 'You're going to have to tell him – there's no way round it, is there? And if you don't, there's plenty will.'

'Not plenty – just that interfering old bitch Madge Fitzgerald.' Grace got up and paced the room, wringing her hands. 'I dunno what she gets out of trying to make everyone else's life a misery.'

She'd heard a few mutterings among her neighbours of

course, when she was carrying Barbara, *husband long gone*. All the gossips made merry. But it was only Mrs Fitzgerald from along the street, with her religious airs and graces, who might feel it her bounden duty to come out with it to Ted's face. Just as she was the one who had stopped Grace in the street when she was six months gone with Barbara. She was a pink-faced woman with big solid legs and a brick-red coat who hadn't even a good word to say about her own husband.

'You needn't think you can hide the fact that you're in the family way,' she said, not troubling to keep her voice down. 'I should've thought you'd be ashamed of yourself, with your husband away, fighting for his country.' For a moment Grace, standing in front of her trembling with shame and fury, thought Mrs Fitzgerald was going to spit in her face. Instead she gave a haughty sniff and walked around Grace, keeping her distance as if Grace had the plague, and sailed along the road like a walking wall.

'I can't tell him – not today. I just can't . . .'

'Look,' Joan interrupted, subsiding heavily onto her chair again. 'You've kept it from Ted – and you've kept it from his mom and dad, up till now. But it can't go on like this. You're going to have to face the music. And if he won't have it – and most husbands wouldn't – well, that'll be how it is. No one'd blame him.' Solemn-faced, she shook her head. 'I don't know what Mom would've said . . .'

'Nor do I, since I never had the benefit of hearing *any-thing* she said,' Grace snapped, seeing where this familiar conversation was going. The old grief filled her for a moment. She and Joan had been brought up by their mother's sister after both their parents were carried off by the Spanish flu in 1918. Grace, who had not even been two years old, could barely remember their mother. It was an absence and loss that haunted her life, despite the

9

kindness of Auntie Rose, until she passed away herself, just before this last war. Grace envied Joan, who was seven when their mom died and had had more of her. Not enough, though, she thought furiously, to take it upon herself to predict all moral judgements that their mother might have handed out to Grace on this subject.

'Look, sis,' she begged. 'I'll tell him – course I will. What else can I do? But just take her for me for a day or two, will you? Keep her out of the way? I can't have him turn up and find another man's child in the house, straight away. It's just not right.'

'Well, that's the truth,' Joan said sniffily, but she reached down and stroked Barbara's head. The baby was kicking her legs excitedly. 'Still – you can't unmake this one now, can yer?'

'I know,' Grace said. 'Look, here's her things.' She passed the bag over. 'Thanks, sis.'

'You're not going already, are yer? Don't you want a cuppa now you're here?'

'No – I've got to go and get summat for Ted for dinner . . .' She looked round distractedly. 'God – I'm a bag of nerves. What if . . .' She didn't want to say it. *What if I don't recognize him? I can hardly remember what he looks like* . . . Even with their wedding picture on the mantel, the picture she has stared at and kissed goodnight for so many years, of the shy bridegroom who had stood beside her.

'What about . . . I mean . . .' Joan hesitated, blushing. 'You're still feeding her?'

Grace, who had been moving towards the door, looked desperately at the clock. It was half past two.

'There's a bottle in the bag. I've put some stera in, watered down. I'll come back later if I can – and I'll be round in the morning, soon as I can. You'll just have to manage . . .'

Joan gave her a very direct look. 'Grace, what I mean is – he's going to notice.'

Grace blushed in turn. Even now, her blouse sometimes got soaked when the milk let down.

'What else can I do? Just take care of her, sis, please.' She looked at her sister again. 'Norm won't say anything, will he?'

It's all right for you, she wanted to say to Joan. *Having your husband here all the time.* Norman worked at Belliss and Morcom making engines and boilers for the navy. Cocky Norman, a skilled man in a reserved occupation. Ted had always felt inferior to him when they were younger – less skilled, less of a man somehow. Grace knew it was another reason he had volunteered so early for the army.

'He won't. He's under orders,' Joan said. More gently she added, 'Go on – go and get ready for your husband. What'll be will be.'

Grace's eyes filled with tears. She knelt and kissed Barbara, who was absorbed with little Davey. 'See you soon, babby.' She looked up at her sister. 'Her little dolly's in the bag.'

'*Go*,' Joan repeated, tears in her own eyes now. 'She'll be all right with me. Just sod off home and sort yourself out, eh?'

Three

Grace raced to the shops. It was late in the day and there was no fresh meat left. She resorted to a tin of bully beef and added veg for a stew, trying to steady herself with the routine of cooking.

Once the smell of meat and gravy was stealing through the house, she went upstairs. With trembling hands, feeling like a criminal, she packed away Barbara's few clothes, her napkins and toys, into the chest of drawers in the back bedroom.

Thank goodness Nora's already gone, she thought. Nora, a girl from near Belfast, with rusty-brown hair, watery blue eyes and a sweet nature, had lodged with her for much of the war while she worked in munitions. She had been a godsend in terms of rent and company and moral support. But now she was married to a lad she had met in Birmingham, and had moved on.

Grace had been fond of Nora but it would have been very awkward now if Nora was still here. It was hard enough knowing how things were going to be with Ted . . .

Guiltily, she searched every room for any of Barbara's things – a muslin cloth here, a nappy pin there – until she was sure there was nothing lying about.

It won't be for long, she thought, one way or another. She didn't let her mind follow the path of what might happen . . .

It did not take long to hide every trace of her small

daughter. With a pang she thought of Barbara sleeping at Joan's tonight. Her baby had spent every night of her life until now tucked up in bed here beside her, in her bedroom – hers and Ted's.

She went into her bedroom, which was at the front, looking out over the street. At this time of day Grace was usually taken up with Barbara. But today, with the dinner cooked and ready, she couldn't think of anything else to do, and now the nervous tension of waiting overtook her completely.

Sitting on the side of the bed, she took a deep breath. Her heart was pounding. The window was open a crack and she could hear children, a bouncing ball, a motorbike passing.

Ted. Ted's coming home . . . It was so hard to believe.

If she had not had Barbara, how different this homecoming would have been. All the longing she had felt for him and all the lost days would just have fallen away. She could have run into his arms with no worry or shame, as she had done when they were first together. She had known Ted since she was seventeen, the quiet, handsome boy she met after he had come to Ladywood to work at the sawmill. They had met at a hop in a church hall and he was so shy she had to ask him to dance in the end.

Tears rose in her eyes, thinking of it. God, she thought, how innocent we both were. It had been a few years until they started walking out seriously. They had seen each other on and off in groups of friends. Lots of girls liked the look of Ted. He was tall and thin, with curly brown hair and grey eyes which smiled even when he wasn't saying much. A few years later, both more grown-up, or so it seemed then, they had got to know each other again. He was still at the sawmill; she was working in a haberdashery

13

shop near Five Ways. The first time he kissed her properly, he was trembling.

Laying one hand on the bed, she stroked the coverlet, remembering. All those nights they had lain here. Nights they had fallen into bed exhausted, other nights making love, drifting into sleep at last, holding hands. And then, as time passed, Ted sleeping beside her as she lay staring up into the dark wondering in silent desperation why, after all these months of marriage, she had still not caught for a baby.

They never talked about it, not properly. If she raised it, Ted blushed and said something like, 'Ah well – I s'pose it takes a while.'

But how long is a while, she would think. She loved him for not blaming her the way she blamed herself. She tried not to show it, but by the time they had been married for more than two years and still there was no sign of a child, she felt desperate. What were they doing wrong? Was there something the matter with her? She couldn't even bear to talk to Joan about it – Joan who by then had two kids with her smug, chirpy husband. Who could you go to to find out? She couldn't face asking Dr. Miles. The very thought made her blush. And she was afraid that Ted was angry with her. He had married a barren woman. Wasn't that what it was called – like in the Bible? And didn't that mean a failed woman?

It was only when Ted joined up, suddenly, in 1939, that she caught a glimmer of how he felt.

'I've always been useless at everything,' he said. 'School – never was any good there. That's why I went to the sawmill – at least I could be outside and not have to write and that. At least this is something I can do.' He had taken her in his arms after telling her he had joined up, and now he looked earnestly down at her. 'I need to do

14

summat to feel like a man, Gracie. And they say it'll all be over in a few months – I'll soon be back.'

Over. It was over for Ted all right, his testing of his manhood. Amid all the heroes of Dunkirk with their little boats and astonishing escapes from the beach-head, there were those lads of the British Expeditionary Force who did not reach British shores. Grace had waited, praying, as trainload after trainload of men were delivered back to their homes. After an agonizingly long wait her prayers were answered by a letter from Ted saying he had been captured. He was a prisoner of war.

She had the small bundle of his letters. She realized they hardly told her anything. He was so bad at writing, couldn't spell, It was as if he seized up with a pen in his hand. *Deer Grace, I am al rit. Not il or anithing. The das goe sloly. The othr lads ar al rit. Lov Ted.* It almost made her laugh when she received them, how the letters left her almost as much in the dark as before. But at least he was alive. He was safe and out of the fighting.

She sat trying to remember the best of him. His laughing eyes and steady ways. His kindness and modesty. Never anything cocky about Ted. But a chill stab of fear went through her. Ted was very straight. Very moral. There he was, all this time, held prisoner. And she . . .

Shame washed through her. The thought of *him* returned to her, uninvited, but with a flicker of longing. *He*, who had given her Barbara, whose lively, muscular body had brought something back to life in hers . . .

'For God's sake!' She leapt up from the bed and stood in front of the cheval mirror in the corner. In front of her she saw a petite, thin woman, her curly black hair falling over her shoulders, with full lips and hollow eyes, the dark brows pulled into a frown. 'Stop thinking about him,' she scolded her reflection. 'Pull yourself together.

You're never going to see him again. Ted – your lovely husband Ted – is coming home and you are his wife. And by God, you owe him.'

She selected from the cupboard an old favourite dress that she knew Ted liked. It was royal blue, but it hung on her now she had lost weight. Joan, always of a bigger build, had not changed size much during the war and having Davey, while Grace seemed to have lost the full curves she had had before. She pulled the belt tight round her waist, brushed out her wild hair, pinned it back and touched up her lips with a red lipstick.

She stood looking at herself, her heart thudding, constantly alert for the sound of a knock or the door opening. Why would he knock? It was his house, after all.

Now Barbara was not here she could almost believe that things were as they had been before. Just her and Ted. Husband and wife. If only she could turn back time!

But there was her little Barbara – her beautiful blonde girl. The baby who had showed her that she too could have a child. She just could not seem to have a child with Ted.

Four

He did knock, at last, just as the clocks were striking six.

Grace had been wandering around the house, unable to sit still. She kept checking and checking again for any signs of Barbara in a fever of guilt and worry. Seeing the house as if for the first time: the sagging corner of the ceiling in the back room, the mould patches on the walls, the rotten window frames and the peeling front door that Ted had painted before he left. Every stick of furniture – the table, chairs and sideboard in the kitchen, second-hand to begin with – was now five years older. The house had never been much, but now it looked truly neglected.

But some things were just the same. There were the few pictures on the mantel in the front room – the room she kept nice for sitting in, with the two brown upholstered armchairs by the fire, the little rag rug. There was the portrait of Ted's mom and dad, standing side by side, taken at someone else's wedding. An old picture of her own mother, eternally young and dark-haired, but faded now almost to nothing. And in the middle, the picture of herself and Ted that she had kissed every night. Or, she thought, pierced again by guilt – almost every night.

Every few minutes she went to the window to peer along the street for any sign of him. She was at the back, giving the stew pot another stir, when at last she heard a rap of knuckles on the front door.

Each step she took towards it seemed to take an age.

She could feel everything – the brush of her cotton frock against her skin, the heavy warmth of her hair on the back of her neck, her breaths, which she had to force in and out – highlighted and intense in this moment, in each step towards the door, in her reaching out her hand and pulling it open . . .

A tall, crop-headed, frighteningly thin man stood outside. He was dressed in army uniform with a bag slung from one shoulder. The face was gaunt, sick-looking, the hollow eyes seeming too ashamed to look into hers, yet also wanting to devour the sight of her.

In shock, she clutched the door for support, her legs almost giving way. Ted . . . Was this spectre Ted? The height, the eyes . . . Yes, his eyes, his shape . . .

'Ted?' She needed to hear his voice but could hardly manage to speak herself. Her heart was overflowing with fear, pity and tenderness . . . *Ted, my Ted . . .*

'Gracie?' Yes, yes, it was him, though the voice was low and hoarse. 'You got the telegram?'

'Yes.' They both stood stunned and stupid, staring at each other. Until, her voice rising with emotion, she cried, 'You're back! I thought you were never going to come back . . .' The tears began to run down her cheeks, and sobs which had waited so long she had hardly known they were there burst out of her.

Ted stepped forward and they were both in the house, in the front room, the door shutting, he letting his bag drop to the floor, seizing hold of her and pulling her close with an anguished howl, sobs breaking from him as well.

'Gracie . . . Oh, my Gracie.'

Weeping, he buried his face in her hair, kissed her neck, her face, his hands exploring as if he couldn't believe her, like a starving person finding food. She had never known so much force in him before and she was moved and a bit afraid of this frantic skeleton she held in her arms, surprisingly strong despite his sick appearance. But it was him. He was here, home at last.

'Ted?' She drew back, trying to calm him. She looked into his eyes and stroked his face, which wore a famished expression. Their lips met and then they were on the stairs, then upstairs, he peeling her dress over her head, tugging at his belt, then on the bed and he inside her as if it was the only thing in life he had to do ever again. She felt sharp pains in the back of her thighs and realized it was his hip bones digging into her. It had never been like that before – he was so thin – and she pulled him close and his back felt like a piano, all bones as well. They lay weeping, clinging to each other as if they were afraid all this might disappear again.

'Five years,' he sobbed. 'Five years down the pan. I'm sorry, Gracie. I'm so sorry.' And then all he could do was say her name, Gracie, my lovely Gracie, over and over again.

'Sssh, love.' She held him and stroked him, confused. 'It's not your fault, is it? How could it be your fault? You're home now, Ted. That's all that matters.'

And at that moment that felt like the one thing that was true.

She laid the table for them to eat the meal she had prepared.

'That looks nice,' he said as he sat down, politely, like a guest. He had flung the bag he brought into the wardrobe in their room and changed into his old clothes – grey trousers, a shirt. The clothes hung on him, almost ridiculous. He had to tie the belt because there were not enough holes.

As she spooned out the food she saw him looking around the room, a faint smile on his lips.

'Hasn't changed much, has it?' she said.

Ted shook his head. She saw the muscles move in his scrawny neck. 'No – I s'pose not. Seems astonishing. This house – you, here all the time. It's been the only thing keeping me going.'

'It's the worse for wear. Still standing though – not like some.'

Ted nodded, distantly. 'Yeah – I saw.'

She smiled, looking at his thin, yellow face. If he could only put on some weight, he might look more like the young, fresh-faced Ted she remembered, rather than this wrung-out-looking stranger, who seemed more like a sick old man. And, she thought, with a pang of guilt and terrible dread, he thinks that all this time nothing has changed, that I'm just exactly as I was when he left. And already, now the heat of their hurried reunion had passed, she was frightened. She could feel the tingle of milk letting down in her breasts.

'Well,' she said brightly, across the plates of watery stew and potatoes, 'it'll take a bit of getting used to.'

'Oh – they ain't finished with me yet.' His voice contained more bitterness than she had ever heard before. 'I'm still in the army. I'm on leave, that's all.'

'Oh, Ted.' She put down her knife and fork. She had hardly taken this in, had thought of him as being home for good. 'But the war's over . . .'

'Not in the east. They reckon they're training us up. They want us to go back and . . .'

He couldn't speak. He stared down at his plate and to Grace's horror she saw tears begin to run down his cheeks again. He put his elbows on the table, hands over his face.

'Ted?' Moved, she got up and went to him, putting her

arms round his shoulders, shocked again by his boniness. 'What is it, love?'

'I can hardly cross the road.' His shoulders were shaking. 'I come up here from the tram stop and I stood there . . . Took me ages just to . . . I can't . . . And they want to send us off to God knows where . . .' He wept and shook for a moment and she held him, helpless and appalled.

'Sorry. I'm sorry . . .' He drew his forearms across his eyes, almost angrily, one after another. 'I feel wet, so useless . . . I can't seem to stop doing this. I just . . . I don't know how to live any more . . .'

'Oh, love.' She held him and kissed him again before sitting down. 'It must be ever so hard.' She spoke cautiously, not really knowing at all, wondering what she should ask. They were talking across a gulf of time apart and hardly knew where to begin.

'How – I mean, when did you get here? Have you come from . . . ?' France, she assumed.

'They brought us back a month ago or so,' he said, staring at his plate. 'I've just come up from down south.'

'A *month*?' She stared at him. She couldn't take in what he meant. 'What d'you mean – you've been in the country . . . ?'

Ted was nodding. 'They put me in hospital.'

'You mean, here, in England?' She felt appalled, terribly wounded. 'But why daint you tell me – let me know? I could've . . .'

'No.' He cut her off. He seemed unable to meet her eyes. 'No. I were in no state. I daint want you to see me – not like that. It's bad enough now.'

She was silenced by the force in his voice. It stopped her asking more. She felt full of dread. What on earth had happened to him to make him like this? But she couldn't ask now. Maybe they should just talk about everyday things.

'I expect you'll want to see your mom and dad soon?' she said carefully. Mr and Mrs Chapman lived a few miles away in Highgate. Grace had continued to go and see them from time to time – without Barbara. They didn't know about Barbara either.

Ted nodded. 'Yeah. Tomorrow.' She saw him make a huge effort to gather himself and ask her. 'Tell me how's everyone – Joan and Norm and the family?'

Five

They had made love again in the dark, when they went to bed. But throughout the night, Ted twitched and fidgeted beside her. Agitated, he talked in his sleep, in what seemed to be German. Grace kept waking, shocked out of unconsciousness. She had no idea what he was saying but it was so disturbing to hear it coming from Ted, in the dark. Anything in German sounded horrible after all those newsreels they had seen of Hitler's harsh, blustering speeches. It was only in the later part of the night that either of them had a more peaceful rest.

In the morning she woke with another jolt, sitting bolt upright. *Barbara! Why isn't she awake? What's happened?*

Usually the thing that woke her was her daughter's movements and hungry cry, here in her bed. Instead, her breasts were taut with milk and beside her was the large sleeping shape of a man . . . She had to remind herself that this foreign body beside her was her husband.

Ted! My Ted – he's home! For a moment she was overcome with excitement, with joy. After all this time when she had begun to think he would never come, her husband was here and they could live again.

And then all the confusion and dread came pouring back. *Barbara.* What had she done – what had she allowed to happen? Something that could never be undone. How could Ted ever forgive her for that? He never could – she could already see.

Oh, Lord, she thought, putting her hands over her face. *What can I do? Help me, please.* She wondered, as she had wondered many times before, whether Joan and Norman could keep Barbara. What if they were to pretend she was theirs? But as well as her sister and brother-in-law, their two older boys already knew perfectly well Barbara was not their sister. How could she wish a life of lies upon them all?

I've got to tell him. She had been round this in her head so many times and always this was what it came back to. The truth.

But I've got to give him time to settle in – to get a bit better. He seems so . . . She turned to look at the emaciated figure lying beside her. He wasn't himself. Ted, on his side, turned away from her, was at last deeply asleep. He had pushed the bedclothes away and was only covered from the waist downwards.

She looked at the back of his head with its cropped brown hair. She could only see the side of his face, the cheekbone jutting out. Who was he, this man who had come home to her? Tears rose in her eyes. Damn this war! Damn all of it, for all the death and destruction and taking loved ones away . . . And now – how could she tell this broken-looking man what she had done, after all he had suffered? She would have to – but not yet. It was impossible.

Carefully, she lay back down again. She studied her husband's bare back, the birthmark to the right of his neck where his collar went, the scattering of little moles across his pale skin. But she glimpsed something new on the shoulder blade closest to the mattress. Peering closely, she could make out a round, rough-edged scar. An old scar, long healed now by the look of it. Recoiling, she lay on her back. What on earth had happened? She had so many questions to ask – but she must not hurry Ted.

A thought forced into her mind. *Him.* She had never studied *his* back in this slow, familiar way. There had never been time. His back had felt stockier, fleshier certainly than Ted's was now. She closed her eyes, remembering, yet willing herself not to remember. April 1944. Where was he now? She had no idea. She must force him out of her mind as she had tried to do all these months and never, ever think of him.

Ted, my husband, is here, she thought, lying in the light of this Tuesday morning, hearing the footsteps of people walking to work outside. *He's home.* Relief filled her, and love and remembering. Her Ted. Then her blood raced again.

Barbara. Oh my God – how am I going to tell him?

The pulsing of her body drove her out of bed. She crept down to put the kettle on. While the water boiled she squeezed milk from her breasts into the sink in the scullery to ease her discomfort. Tears rose in her eyes again as she imagined Barbara crying for her, inconsolable. But Ted mustn't notice – not yet. Not until she had told him. She sank down at the table as the kettle began to murmur, light slanting in through the window. Out at the back they had a little strip of garden – her few vegetables planted to the left. To the right, a patch of rough grass.

A bird was singing. Once, before all this, before the war when she was a different person, that would have sounded so fresh and innocent.

Her heart thudded hard. She would have to find a reason to go out, to run and feed Barbara . . .

Leaning her head in her hands, her black waves of hair falling forward, she sighed from the depths of her. Her mind circled for the umpteenth time. If only everything was different. If it hadn't been for *him*, for that time of weakness, of despair and need of comfort . . . Everything would be different now. She was a terrible, terrible person. What sort of wife allowed herself to get into the situation she had got into while her husband was shut away, wounded, a prisoner, with nothing?

She carried the two cups of tea upstairs. As she came into the room, Ted was lying with his eyes open. He turned to look at her.

'Couldn't think where I was for the life of me, for a minute,' he said, and smiled. For a moment, he looked more like the old Ted and it lifted her spirits.

'I bet,' she said, smiling back. 'Home in your own bed. Here – I made us some tea.' She climbed in beside him, the brass bedstead creaking.

'Just need to go . . . You know.' He jerked his head towards the privy out the back and flung back the bed-clothes. Grace gasped in horror.

'Ted – what the hell's happened to your feet?'

There were toes missing on each foot. Both big toes were intact, though they were a deep, grim-looking purple. Each foot was a mess of dark, discoloured stumps. Even the few remaining parts of the toes were plum-coloured, corrupted-looking things.

'Oh ah,' he said, with a bitter kind of casualness. 'Yeah – lost them in Germany.' He flung his legs over the side of the bed, his back to her, thin body curved like a bow. 'Makes it difficult to balance sometimes.'

Heart pounding, she watched as he limped to the door. It felt as if he was a thousand miles away still, even though he was here.

Six

She was afraid Ted would insist on her going with him to see his mother and father. It would all be a lie, her having to pretend again because of Barbara. She desperately didn't want to go. But Ted seemed brighter this morning.

'No I'll go,' he said. 'Got to try and get used to things.'

'They'll be dying to see you,' she said, on tenterhooks to get to Barbara. If only he'd get going!

But he sat on at the table, smoking one cigarette after another and seemingly in a world of his own. Eventually, when she had busied herself with breakfast and washing-up, she could stand it no longer.

'I've just got to pop down the shops for a few things,' she said. She gave him a peck on the cheek. 'Won't be long.'

She tore down the street, patches of wetness seeping through the cotton of her blouse. After this longest ever separation she was desperate to see Barbara, convinced that her little girl would have been crying for her all night, or that something awful would have happened.

She burst into her sister's house. 'Joan?'

'Here.'

There was no sound of any crying. In the kitchen she found Joan at the table with Davey on the floor and Barbara in her lap, looking perfectly cheerful. For a second Grace felt hurt. Barbara appeared to be quite happy without her.

'She been all right?' she panted.

'Course. Look, Baba – who's here?' She handed the little girl over and Grace settled down to feed her. It was a lovely relief to hold her in her arms again.

'She was a bit restless at first – daint want the bottle, after you, but she took it in the end. She's been a little darlin' for me, haven't you?' She stroked the baby's face with her finger and sat down again, her face serious. 'So – how's Ted?'

The tears that had been waiting all morning came pouring out then.

'I don't know,' Grace sobbed. 'Oh, Joan – he hardly looks like my Ted any more. He's so thin and he just sits there staring as if he's a million miles away. And some of his toes've dropped off . . .'

'*What?*'

'He said . . . I don't know. He won't say anything hardly.' She wiped her own tears from Barbara's plump cheek. 'Summat about losing them in Germany. I mean, I'm glad to have him home, course I am. But I don't know where to start with him . . . Let alone her . . .' She looked down at her contented child. 'He's going over to see his mom and dad. Or he said he was. Daint seem to want to move.'

After a moment Joan said, 'Well, he's bound to have to adjust. I 'spect he just needs things to get back to normal. It's been a long time. Tell you what, when Norm gets in, we'll pop round and see you both. Pol and Jen, the little wenches next door, are mad about babbies – they'll pop round for a bit and stay with her and Davey. I 'spect Ted needs to see people – like before. Take him out of himself.'

'All right,' Grace said. She felt a bit doubtful as to how happy Ted was going to be to see Norm, who had been

28

tucked up at home doing the same job all through the war, but she knew Joan was trying to help.

'And this one'll be all right for a day or two with me,' Joan went on. 'It'll be good for her, taking from the bottle. It'll help with weaning her off you.'

Grace looked at her sister's homely face and felt a surge of fondness and gratitude.

'Thanks, sis. It's not everyone'd do this . . . Not after, you know . . .'

'After you carrying on like a flaming idiot with no sense, you mean?' Joan looked severely at her.

'Something like that, yeah.' Grace lifted Barbara, who had finished feeding, and cuddled her. 'Everyone makes mistakes,' she said defensively. It sounded feeble even as she said it.

'Yes – and some of them are flaming bigger ones than others.'

'All right, all right.' She had heard this many times before and didn't want to hear yet again the lecture about how foolish and disgraceful she was – as if she didn't know. 'I'll go and change her and then I'd better get back.' She looked at Joan. 'Thanks, sis.'

Grace hurried back to Inkerman Street via the shops. When she got in, Ted was not there. She was worried by how much this filled her with relief.

Another thought chilled her, though. Who might Ted meet while he was out? Mrs Fitzgerald? Pray God, no. His other pals. Larry and Ern and that lot – well, Ern was away in the army himself and Larry – she hadn't seen him in a very long time. None of them knew about Barbara. She found herself checking off anyone they knew, anyone who might say anything. There were only a couple of girls at the factory where she had worked who knew she was expecting – and people close by in the neighbour-hood. She'd just have to hope none of them would say anything to him. She breathed a little more easily.

She did her bits of housework quickly, with no baby interruptions. The house felt very empty without Barbara. She had already readied the place for Ted's arrival yesterday and apart from sweeping out the downstairs room, wiping the table and peeling the last few spuds, there was not much to do. Needing to keep busy, she hand-washed the clothes Ted had taken off and took them outside to hang up.

The garden was a little strip with the brick privy just outside to the right. At the far end was a rough wall against which leaned the remains of an old wooden pigeon coop left by the previous occupant. The rest was mostly grass, except for her little patch where she had dug for victory and planted vegetables along the dilapidated fence.

As she hung out Ted's shirt she took deep breaths of the morning air, looking across at the blue slate rooftops of the neighbouring Ladywood street. She could feel the milk gathering in her breasts again, the thud of her blood. Every part of her felt tense, her stomach turning queasily. *Help me, someone . . .*

She could hear women's voices from a couple of gardens away, two of her neighbours canting over the wall. She thought she could just make out Mrs Fitzgerald's snooty tones, gossiping as usual, and Grace retreated quickly inside.

She was thinking about putting the dinner on when there was a knock at the door. On the step she found Ted. For a second it was almost as strange as the first time.

'What're you knocking for?' she asked, with a nervous laugh. 'This is your house.'

'I dunno,' he said, stepping in. 'It just feels funny, that's all.'

'I'm making dinner.' She had watered down the stew again, added a bit of turnip. Everything they ate was about eking out. She made busy at the stove. 'We must get your ration book. How're your mom and dad?'

'Oh, all right, yeah,' Ted said. He stood in the kitchen, hands pushed into his pockets, a long sagging figure. 'Yeah, they're all right.'

He had never been a great talker but this was different. He seemed utterly lost in his own home.

'I saw Joan,' Grace said, keeping her voice light, as if everything was normal. She lifted the pan of boiled potatoes to drain them. 'She said they'd pop over later.'

'Cooee – it's me – and Norm!' She heard Joan's voice at the front when it was already evening, the light beginning to fade.

'Come in!' Grace called, relieved to have other company.

While she and Ted ate their dinner together earlier, Grace had made bright attempts at conversation, asking more about Mr and Mrs Chapman and saying, without really meaning it, that she should go and see them soon too. But his replies were so brief that soon silence fell again. Ted seemed exhausted by his morning's activity and as soon as he had finished eating, he went up and lay on the bed.

Grace didn't know what to do with herself. She was used to her day revolving round Barbara's needs. She thought about running to Joan's again, but knew she shouldn't. She crept up and got on the bed beside Ted. For a moment she sat looking down at his face. The sight of him filled her with tenderness mixed with dread. She lay down, listening

31

to his loud breathing as her mind spun and spun. At last she dozed for a while, then woke, bewildered.

The afternoon had crawled by, full of the distant sound of children playing outside.

Now Ted was downstairs again and she had reminded him Joan and Norm were coming. It was reassuring to see her sister's plump form in the doorway in her yellow frock printed with flowers. Her hair was loose and rolled and pinned back from her forehead. She thought guiltily how tired Joan looked, bags under her eyes.

Their eyes met – *is Barbara all right?* – and Joan gave a tiny nod back, her lips flicking into a smile for a second.

Norm was a small, compact man, no taller than his wife. His brown hair was slicked back, sleeves rolled. He had a round, pink face and was perpetually cheerful. Today, though, Grace could see that he looked uneasy and her stomach tightened with worry. Surely Norm wouldn't say anything about Barbara, would he? Not now?

Ted got slowly to his feet. Grace could see it cost him effort. She watched nervously.

'Hello, Ted,' Joan said, coming and kissing him. She held his arms and looked warmly at him. 'It's nice to have you back with us, love. It's been a very long time.'

'Ta, Joanie,' Ted said. He managed a smile. He and Joan had always got along. He looked over her shoulder, saying, 'All right, Norm?' Grace could hear the wariness in his voice.

'All right, lad?' Norm said breezily, advancing on him as Joan stepped out of the way. 'Nice to see you.' With a chuckle he added, 'Back from that holiday camp of yours, then?'

Ted reacted instantly, with full force. He drew his arm back and punched Norm so hard in the jaw that he staggered and fell back into the table. Losing his balance, he slithered to the floor.

'Ted!' Grace cried, horrified. She was amazed that Ted could manage to hit anyone so hard. 'Oh my God, Norm – are you all right?'

'Christ.' Amid the commotion, Norm sat stunned on the floor rubbing his jaw.

Joan reached her hand out to her husband. 'Come on, Norm,' she said quietly. 'Get up.' She looked at Ted warily, but with understanding. 'He daint mean it, did yer, Ted?'

Grace's heart was pounding, her hands clammy. She had never seen her husband behave like this ever before. She was afraid of what was happening, of this new Ted, and of what Norm might say next. *Your wife's bastard child is in our house, Ted, did you know that?*

To her eternal gratitude, Norm did not say it. He got slowly to his feet, still rubbing a hand over his jaw. They all stood round. Ted was quivering, breathing hard, gulping breaths, obviously trying to control his emotions and not succeeding.

'Sorry, pal.' Norm's usually cocky demeanour was subdued for once. 'I never meant . . .'

'Sorry . . .' Ted managed. Grace could hear that he was close to tears. 'I'm just . . . Sorry . . .' He put his head down and hurriedly disappeared out of the back door.

'Look – we'll come back another day,' Joan said. 'What did you have to go and say that for, Norm?'

'I never meant it – it was just a joke.' He shook his head. 'Come on – best get home. See yer, Grace . . .'

'Sorry,' Grace said helplessly. She felt suddenly very afraid. 'He's just a bit . . .'

Joan turned as she and Norm headed out of the door. 'Don't worry, sis. You'll be all right, won't you? But it's best we go, I think. See you soon, eh?'

Grace stood alone in the back room and saw her husband out in the garden, standing alone, thin as a pole, staring ahead of him.

Seven

'Ted?'

Grace spoke into the darkness as she lay beside him that second night. He was lying on his back and she could tell he was not asleep. He had hardly said a word since the incident with Norm.

There was no reply.

'I know you're awake, love.' Her heart was thumping again. She felt so nervous, trying to approach the man she had been married to for almost nine years. It was like trying to break into a locked cupboard.

There was a long silence, which felt to her like being pushed away. Hurt and rejected, she started to cry.

'Oh, Ted,' she sobbed, her head against his shoulder. 'I'm your wife. Why won't you talk to me?'

She felt him breathe in deeply and let out a sigh from the very depths of him.

'I never meant to hit him,' he burst out suddenly. 'It just . . . I dunno. I forgot who I was . . . And he should never've said what he said . . .'

'It's all right.' She stroked his chest with timid fingers, overjoyed to hear him say anything at all. 'Norm was all right. He understands you've been . . .' She trailed off. Been what? She had no real idea. 'Ted – can't you talk to me? Tell me what's happened?'

He sat up in bed so suddenly that his elbow collided with the side of her head, hurting her.

'What's happened?' His voice rang out like a shout in the quiet. 'Five years of my life's what's happened. Five years of my bloody useless life down the pan. And now I'm . . .'

Cutting himself off, he climbed out of bed.

'Ted,' she begged, crying all the more because it almost felt as if he had hurt her on purpose. He was pulling on his trousers. 'Don't – it's late – where're you going?'

'I dunno. Out. To 'ave a bit of peace.'

He picked up his shoes and stormed downstairs. A few moments later she heard the front door bang.

After crying herself out, Grace slept for a time. But she did hear Ted come back, what felt like an age later, and slide into bed beside her. She was up long before him the next morning, dashing to Joan's to feed and cuddle Barbara before Ted was even awake.

'You look terrible,' Joan observed.

'Yeah. Well.'

She felt too low and exhausted to talk. Her head was throbbing. She looked down at Barbara, pink and lovely, enjoying her morning feed. If only she could just go somewhere quiet and peaceful, just her and her little girl. All these years longing for Ted to come home and now he was here, it would have felt easier if he had not come back. Shame washed through her. What a terrible thing, to be thinking that it might have been easier to be a widow.

'He'll settle down,' Joan said cautiously.

She didn't ask Grace when she was going to tell Ted about the baby.

He appeared downstairs at about eleven, just as she got back from the shops. It felt easier to be out, to keep moving, to stand in a queue with the usual ration hunters, complaining about how were they supposed to put a meal on the table every day. There must still be a handful of spuds left in the garden, she was thinking as she emptied her shopping bag of tiny rations of cheese and meat.

And there he was, standing by her, looking terrible, like a beaten dog.

'I'm sorry, Grace.' Tears started to run down his face and his shoulders were shaking. 'I'm sorry . . .'

They held each other then, both crying. And then in the middle of it, Ted pushed her away, gently, but as if he could not manage any more, and wiped his face roughly.

'What's to eat?' he said. His voice was rough as well.

Somehow they lived through those first days.

Grace found excuses to be out first thing – she must go to the shops, deliver something to a friend, take something to Joan . . . Ted was sleeping badly so he was often still in bed until late into the morning and Grace could dash to Joan's and back without him noticing. He needed to rest nearly all the time.

They moved around each other. Some nights, they made love in the dark of their bed, without speaking. Grace ached with missing Barbara. She tried to keep cheerful, to be kind, heartbroken as she felt.

She kept telling herself that she must give Ted time. Whatever had happened to him, he needed to get used to being at home. And she was his wife. She had done a terrible thing. The least she could do was to look after him.

Eight

For most of that first week, Ted didn't go out. He slept, he sat, he stood in the garden for many minutes at a time, staring at nothing in particular. He smoked. Grace started to feel she would go mad. If only he had to go to work! The old days of Ted disappearing every morning in his dark-blue overalls, a jacket slung over the top, with a packet of sandwiches and a bottle of tea, seemed like heaven. Everything before the war, when things were right and there were no lies or secrets, seemed like a dream now.

She felt lonelier than she had ever been during the war. Then, she had had Nora living here, good-natured and easy-going. There were the other girls at work. But now, she felt alone and weighed down.

So that when, on Friday, Ted suddenly announced he was going to see his friend Larry (something Grace had suggested umpteen times to no avail), it seemed like a wonderful development. Up until now he had not even told his pals he was home.

'That's a good idea,' she said, her heart lifting with relief. Surely this was a good sign? Larry had spent the war at Bulpitts, a factory that had gone over to war production.

The morning was crawling past. She had done her usual dash over to Barbara early on, cleaned the house, and moved around Ted as he sat in the armchair in the back room, huddled up under the rug looking frozen, even though the day was sunny outside. She was getting desperate to get out of the house again herself.

'I need to go to the shops,' she said, glad of a truthful excuse to get out. Cautiously she suggested, 'You could go and dig up the last few spuds. Might warm you up a bit.'

To her relief, Ted seemed pleased by this suggestion.

'Least I can do summat useful,' he said. His voice was bitter but he tried to smile.

As he stood up, the bits of change in his pocket slipped out, sliding down into the back of the chair.

'Oh, *blast* it . . .' He was angry out of proportion to the annoyance, rummaging furiously in the chair, drawing out pennies and a threepenny bit. 'There was a shilling in there . . . Ah – here we go . . .' Hand thrust down the back of the seat, he felt around, frowning. At last he pulled out the shilling, accompanied by something soft and white. 'What's this, then?'

Grace, who had been gathering up her shopping bag and ration books, turned to look. What Ted was holding gave her whole being a jolt, like an electric shock going through her. He was holding a white knitted bootee, one of Barbara's that she had worn through the winter. Grace stared in horror at the soft thing in his hand.

'Oh!' To herself she sounded terribly flustered. 'Well – it's a . . . a baby's bootee. It must've been there for ages.' She laughed, trying to sound casual, and came and took it from him. 'Yes – it must have been that time Margaret Jenkins stopped by with her babby – and he's up and running about now!'

Ted shrugged, and she saw he had already lost interest. He headed for the door.

'There's a few spuds left at the far end,' she said. 'Fork's in the privy.'

39

She stood watching him, hand on her heart, thinking, *Oh my Lord, I can't go on like this.*

She walked slowly along Inkerman Street, between the sooty brick faces of the houses, calling greetings to a few of the neighbours. Mrs Astbury, ginger curls peeping out from under a scarf, was sweeping out her front room and she beckoned Grace over.

'All right, are yer? I see you've got your Ted home. All right for some, eh? Dunno when my Len's going to get back. I'm worried they'll just send him over there next – you know, out east.'

Grace forced a smile. She knew that Win Astbury had not set eyes on her husband for four years. Their son, Billy, was seven now. He would hardly remember a thing about his father. Win always managed to keep cheerful somehow, though.

'Yes, ta, Win,' she said, wanting to seem in good spirits. 'He's been back a few days. He's only on leave, though – they might post him out there as well.'

Mrs Astbury tutted. 'Wicked, it is. They ought to send someone else, that's what I think any'ow. Not that anyone ever asks me.'

Grace managed a smile. 'Billy all right?'

'Oh, 'e's all right. Always is – 'e's a good lad. What about your little 'un?' She gave Grace a meaningful look, but there was no malice in it.

'She's doing well, ta,' Grace said, backing away. 'Anyhow – best get to the shops before it's all gone.'

Win Astbury rolled her eyes. 'It's worse now than when it was still going on.' She picked up her broom. 'Bring me back summat nice!'

They both laughed, knowing there was no hope of this. Grace hurried along the road, keeping a sharp eye out for

Mrs Fitzgerald. She walked up Monument Road, past the church and the baths, and queued in various shops. After a long wait she managed, with a sense of triumph, to buy a few tomatoes.

'T'ra!' she called to the greengrocer, stepping out into the sunshine with her bag. 'Ta very much.'

And for the second time that day, she received a shock that jangled through her whole body and caught her breath. Only this time it was even worse. She ground abruptly to a halt.

Walking along the road away from her, on the opposite side, was a man in a navy-blue fireman's uniform. This in itself was not surprising. The fire station was not far away, round the corner. But the walk, the set of the man, was immediately familiar. No. It couldn't be. What was he doing here? He didn't come from Birmingham. He had been sent away, to where she did not know. The one thing she had known was that she would never, ever see him again.

She narrowed her eyes, her breathing jagged. Was she going mad, imagining things?

No. It was definitely him. The fireman who for those few crazy days when he was still in Birmingham had been her friend, and, without her ever deciding on it, her lover.

It was *him*. It was Johnny Duke.

II

Nine

'He's sorry, Norm, he really is,' Grace appealed the next morning, as she sat feeding Barbara at her sister's house. 'He never meant it.'

'I know,' Norm said gruffly. Norm was a cocky so-and-so, but in the end, he was also a kind man. They were at the table in the back, and Ronnie and Joe, their older lads aged eight and six, were playing in the yard. A ball kept thudding against the door. 'His nerves are on edge – you can see. He looks terrible. What the hell's been going on?'

Grace shrugged. 'He won't say. He's been in a camp in Poland is all I know. How the hell did they get to Poland anyway? He's been poorly, I know that.' She didn't want to mention the wound on Ted's shoulder, or his shouting in German. That felt like telling Norm too much.

She looked across at her sister and brother-in-law with pleading eyes. 'You can see why I can't tell him yet, though, can't you?'

Joan and Norman exchanged a look.

'Thing is, sis,' Joan said carefully, 'how long d'you think you can keep this up for? He's got to know and the longer you keep him in the dark – well, he's going to feel even worse when you come out with it.'

Norm was nodding. 'It ain't right, Grace.'

Shamed, Grace looked down at her lovely child, hugging her close. Barbara was discreetly covered by her cardigan, eyes just peeping out as she fed contentedly, her fingers gripping the edge of the cardigan. Grace seemed to be suffering from the separation far more than Barbara.

'*She's* all right,' Joan said as if reading her mind. 'But you can't go on like this. He's your husband, Grace – and you know what's going to happen. If you don't tell him, someone else will.'

Grace nodded, looking up at her sister again.

'All right,' she said. 'I will. Just give me a day or two – please.'

As she hurried back along the street, all the turmoil of her feelings rose in her. Joan and Norm barely knew the half of her shame and confusion. They did not know that yesterday she had seen Johnny Duke. They had no idea that as she made her way to the shops, and stood wearily waiting in the queues, that Johnny, the father of her child – sunny Johnny with his fair hair, his carefree laugh and strong, energetic body – had forced himself so powerfully into her mind that she could barely think of anything else.

Ted came home from seeing Larry seeming more cheerful.

'The lad's got a good collection of birds there,' he said as they ate the last garden potatoes and a tough bit of fish that Grace had managed to buy. 'He's good with 'em. Real beauties, some of them.'

'I daint think you went in for pigeons and all that,' Grace said carefully.

Ted chewed slowly – it seemed to her he did everything much more slowly these days – and rested his elbows on the table. His arms looked all bone and seemed longer than she remembered.

'No – but I might now. Larry's got a good bunch of lads round him – other fanciers. And he's even got a couple of them Rollers. Beautiful birds, they are.'

He took another mouthful and a silence descended which lasted so long that she thought he had said all he was going to say. But then he nodded towards the window looking over the garden.

'I'll get mending that coop that we've got down there. All it needs is a bit of sorting out.'

'But you're going away again – after your leave?' she said, wondering if he had forgotten.

'Oh ah – I know. But I can get it ready, can't I?' He looked away then, as if closing down the conversation.

'Oh yes! Course you can,' she agreed hastily. She was glad. It would give him something to do.

But as Ted finished his meal, looking down at his plate, terrible thoughts came to her. What if, instead of her sitting here with Ted, she was with Johnny? What if it was cheerful Johnny sitting in front of her every day – and with Barbara here too? A family – tied by blood. Didn't they really belong together?

Horrified at herself, she tried to push the thoughts away. She got to her feet and on the way to the stove, touched Ted on the shoulder. The encouraging words she had been about to say were silenced by his jumping as if she had stuck a pin in him.

'Oh!' He put his hands on his chest, panting. 'Oh God, don't ever do that.'

'Sorry, love. I daint mean . . .' Tears rose in her eyes. Whatever was wrong with him? What had turned her calm, gentle husband into this wreck of a man, living on his nerves? She banished her tears. He didn't mean it.

'I was just going to say – about the pigeons. That sounds like a nice idea.'

There was such a barrier around him that she did not dare ask anything when they were face to face in the daytime.

Only in the dark of the bedroom did she try. It was easier when she could not see him, when she could try to imagine that he still looked like the man she had married. Even his voice was a little bit different – weaker, more tentative. But she could pretend . . .

'When you were in the camp, in Poland,' she had tried last night, feeling as if she was walking across a thinly frozen pond where she might fall in at any moment, 'what did you have to do?'

'All sorts,' Ted said tersely. 'Worked in a sawmill at one time.' He started to laugh, just for a moment, and she stroked her hand gently over his body, snuggling closer to him.

'Well, you'd have known what to do,' she said.

'Worked on farms. One job, we was in a factory, boiling up beets. Great vats of 'em.'

'What for?' She had never heard of beets.

'Sugar.' She felt him shrug slightly, because it seemed obvious to him. 'They look like parsnips. My hands've never been the same since. I did farm work. And in a brickyard.'

She listened, trying to imagine, just happy that he was talking, even if it did not tell her much.

'What happened to your shoulder, love?' she dared to ask.

'Bullet,' he said. 'That was back in '40. On the way there.'

She waited for more but nothing came.

'When did you get let out?' she tried.

'January 23rd.' His voice was clipped now, as if he was reaching the end of his ability to talk.

Grace was bewildered. January? What had taken them so long? 'How did you get back from Poland?'

There was a silence, before Ted said quietly, 'How d'yer think? We walked.'

He turned away from her then, without another word. Once he was sleeping, Grace lay awake, staring up into the dark, feeling as if her husband, though only inches away, was still in a different country.

And *his* face kept coming into her mind, no matter how hard she tried to stop it. His face, with his fair hair, like Barbara's.

Ten

She first met Johnny after work on a snowy night in March 1944. The other girls at the factory were always on at her to come out with them. Grace did go sometimes, for a drink and a natter in a nearby pub. But she never went dancing or anything like that, even though Nora had invited her a few times.

Nora, nineteen when she arrived from Belfast to fill shells for the war effort, was more of a home bird anyway and they had spent most of their nights in, the house swathed in blackout, drinking cocoa and nattering by the fire. It would have felt wrong to go dancing. Grace thought, how could she get up and stand in the arms of another man when she was married? That would have felt disloyal to Ted, and she knew somehow that he would have minded.

The sky was a sombre grey as they left the factory that afternoon, the streets full of slow-falling flakes.

'Come on, Gracie,' her work pal Margaret urged as they moved among the crowds coming off the afternoon shift. It was freezing out. Everyone was pulling up their collar. Margaret was petite as a sparrow, with beautiful dark-eyed looks. 'You can't just sit in all your life, married or not! We're going to make a night of it – go into Birmingham – Steven's Bar. Might be a night they have some drink in.' She made a comical face. Supplies of beer were so uncertain that you had to plump for a time when

50

there might be some in and hope for the best. 'Come on, get yer glad rags on and come with us for once.'

'What – in this?' Grace frowned at the sky. Snowflakes tickled her cheeks.

'It'll be all right. It's only a bit. Come on, Grace. You hardly ever go out.'

It was true. And for once Grace thought, oh, to hell with it.

She had almost forgotten that she was beautiful, or could be. By then, Ted had been away for so long.

The early part of the war had meant so many broken nights of bombing, ack ack guns going and the sound of planes drilling terror into your nerves. And for her it had meant all those weeks of not hearing from Ted after he was captured, not knowing, almost too afraid to think what might have happened. It was September 1940 before she heard from him through the Red Cross. Life had been too difficult and relentless to think about how else it might be. It was a case of getting through from one day to the next, fraught and exhausted as the city was smashed up around you; of wondering whether you would be alive when the dawn broke.

After the bombing died down later in 1941, things had settled into a routine of drab hard work, of sitting in either her blacked-out house with Nora, or sometimes at Joan and Norm's; of rationed food, and shortages of the most basic things like a bar of soap or stockings; of more exhaustion and the boredom and frustration of never knowing when it was going to end.

At least Ted's safe, she had kept telling herself. He's out of it. I know where he is. His brief letters confirmed that much, even if they did not tell her more. *Lov Ted* was his most effusive way of telling her anything he felt. Every night she kissed the man standing beside her in their wedding portrait and tried desperately to remember the sound of his voice, the feel of his arms around her, the dreams they had shared. She knew she had loved him, that she still did. She hoped and prayed, trying to keep the closeness of him alive.

By March 1944 he had been away for more than four years – longer than their married life before he joined up. More and more, as the months went on, she felt as if her young life was passing her by. If she and Ted had not managed to have a child before, how was she ever going to have a family now? The war was stopping that happening – perhaps forever.

And in all that time there had been no one to put their arms around her and tell her they loved her, that she was beautiful. She wondered now if there ever would be again.

The top of the building that held Steven's Bar was bomb-damaged, but the pub had gone on trading on the ground floor. There was a fire in the grate, the windows were all blacked out, and it was cosy and getting quite hot and full of a beery fug. As she sipped her half of watery ale, Grace could feel her cheeks turning pink from the drink and the cold night outside.

He was with a group of lads who came into the crowded pub. Grace and Margaret and their group of girls were crushed in on one side of the noisy room, not far from the bar. Grace was chatting to a girl called Angie about her boyfriend who was in the navy. Angie was a plump blonde girl with a plaintive voice.

'I don't know if 'e'll come back to me,' she was saying. 'I mean we was only going out for three weeks before 'e left, but I liked him. 'E were nice. 'E's writ me once or twice, but . . . Eh, Grace, ain't you got nice hair?'

She reached out to touch Grace's crow-black locks, as if seeing her for the first time. They wore snoods at work to cover their hair.

Grace had pinned her black, tumbling waves of hair back from her face. They lay over her shoulders and the deep-red blouse she was wearing with a black skirt. They were the warmest clothes she had.

'Oh,' she said, 'ta. But your hair's nice – it's pretty.'

As they were talking, one of the lads pushed through towards the bar. He elbowed her in the back by mistake and she couldn't help saying, 'Ow – watch it!'

'Oh – sorry!' As he turned, Grace saw a lad with a strong frame, cropped fair hair and a wide, pleasant face.

'S'all right,' she said.

Angie was still chattering on to her, but soon the lad was back carrying drinks for his group of friends. This time, their eyes met and he smiled. As he crossed the room, she couldn't help watching him. He had the almost swaggering walk of a man with strong leg muscles. He was broad across the shoulders. As she looked he leaned to put the drinks down amid cheers from the others, then turned and looked back, and she knew, when his eyes found her again, that he was looking for her. Blushing, she turned away.

She couldn't seem to help herself. It was as if something in her had been sparked awake again. Through all the other talk of the evening she was aware of the lad, out of the corner of her eye, and every so often she saw him looking at her. Uneasily, she fingered her wedding ring, reminding herself. She was not in a position to go looking at other men.

Before long, though, the lads made their way over, the presence of a group of girls too much of a magnet to resist. And he had made straight for her, as if claiming her.

53

His blatant gaze, even before he had said anything, made her tingle all over, as if she was aware of every inch of her skin against her clothes. She found herself keeping her left hand in her lap.

'Doing all right, are yer?' he said. He was looking at her with such frank admiration that she felt a blush begin in her face and spread down to her chest.

'Yeah, all right,' she said, smiling. He looked nice: friendly and with upturned, laughing lips. His blue eyes also crinkled at the corners as if a smile was always on its way. 'Where're you from then?' – because his accent was different.

'Me? I'm from Leek – Staffs. Us lot . . .' He nodded at the group of lads. 'We're all firemen. I was sent down here to help out when it was bad, like. Still here, though.' He grinned then. 'I like it – it's a bit more lively than where I come from. My name's Johnny, by the way. Johnny Duke.'

'I'm Grace Chapman,' she said.

'You working?' He took a good swig of beer and made a face into the glass. 'More like gnat's pee than ever, this, in't it?'

Grace laughed. 'Yeah. These are my workmates. Some of them, anyway.' She told him where they worked, in Ladywood. 'Making tails for planes.'

She noticed around her that most of the lads had started in on a chat with one of the group of girls, so she did not feel self-conscious.

'I can't see you in a factory,' Johnny said. As he spoke she looked at his strong, masculine hand holding the glass. 'You look like . . . I dunno.' He put his head on one side, and feeling him examining her in such a concentrated way, Grace blushed and giggled. 'You look like a singer. Or an actress.'

'Me?' She laughed. 'I like the odd sing-song – but I'm no singer.'

'Bet you *can* sing,' he said. 'Anyone can. My dad's Welsh – they all sing down there.' He stood tall and for a moment she thought he was about to burst into song, but he seemed to think better of it.

She stayed longer than she meant to. Johnny found a seat next to her later and they chatted on for ages – Johnny telling her about his mom and dad and his sister who was a nurse and his brother who was in the air force, and she told them about Joan and Norm and growing up without a mom and dad. He said he found that really sad and looked genuinely upset for her. And they fell into laughing, easy conversation. But somehow, in all of it, she didn't tell him about Ted, and she guessed later that he never noticed the ring on her finger because if he had he would have said something. And so she always knew it was her fault, all of it. And because the next time she saw him, she had slid the ring off her finger and left it on the chest of drawers in her room. For safekeeping, she told herself.

Some of the other girls peeled off and said they were going home before she did.

'I must go,' she kept saying. The pub crowd was thinning out. Grace had let herself slide into a hazy, dreamy state. She knew she was a bit tiddly, not so much from the watery beer as from this man's eyes on her, the attention he was giving her and his obvious attraction to her.

'I'm off now, Grace,' Margaret said. 'You coming?'

'Yeah, in a minute.' By this time, her eyes and Johnny's seemed almost unable to fix on anything but each other. She just could not pull away.

Margaret soon lost patience and went without her.

'I'll walk you to the bus stop,' Johnny said eventually. She was ashamed that he had to support her as they went out into New Street. She felt unsteady and as if she had entered another life altogether in the last hours. She had forgotten about the war, about work, about Ted. All she could think of was this man, of the desire coursing between the two of them which had heightened as the evening went by.

There was a couple of inches of snow on the ground and its whiteness helped illuminate their way in the blacked-out street. It made the night feel magical. They walked a little way towards her bus, arm in arm. Then without speaking, as if it was the only natural thing to do, he led her into the deeper shadow of the tall buildings and took her in his arms. Their lips met, all cigarettes and beer and forceful hunger. Grace felt as if she had come alive again at last, as Johnny's strong arms pulled her closer to him.

Both of them were breathing heavily as they drew back from each other.

'I've got to go,' she whispered, dazed.

'God, Grace.' She could only see his face in shadowy outline. 'You're a cracker. I noticed you as soon as I came in tonight. When can I see you again?'

That was the moment she could have said it. *It's been nice, but* . . . Instead, she found herself taking in when his days off were, working out where they could meet and, for the remainder of the week until they did, longing for it with a powerful physical longing, even while she told herself that it was all right, they were friends. Just friends. She was a married woman. Nothing was going to happen.

Eleven

Larry Biggins, Ted's pal, arrived at the house on Sunday and started helping Ted fix the pigeon coop. Once they had both had a look at it, it was obvious that the thing was so rotten that they would almost have to start again, so there was much head scratching and chat about where they were going to get anything from to put the thing together. Every sort of material was in short supply.

Larry was a gangly bloke with watery blue eyes, prominent teeth and chaotic muddy-brown hair. He was married to a buxom redhead called Eileen, who, Ted and Grace always used to joke, looked as if she might flatten him. But they seemed a happy pair and Larry was an amiable soul.

In a quiet moment in the kitchen, when Ted had gone out the back for something, Larry turned to Grace.

'When 'e come round ours I nearly never let 'im in – daint know who 'e was.' His distress showed in his eyes and he fidgeted his hand back and forth through his hair. 'Terrible. Gave us a shock, that did.'

'I know,' Grace said. She couldn't speak more because her aching throat seemed to have closed right up and tears filled her eyes.

'Never thought I'd see 'im like this,' Larry said. He looked distraught. ''E won't say what they did to 'em, though. Those *sodding* Krauts.'

She stood at the back door later, the midday sun on her

57

face, voices and digging sounds drifting from the strips of garden stretching away on each side. At the bottom of their garden, Ted and Larry were trying to fix the coop. A length of string was the best they had for the moment. They were like two schoolboys trying to make a go-kart out of nothing and somehow that made her even sadder.

For a moment, she laid a hand over her chest. Over these days since Ted had come home, her milk was gradually beginning to dwindle. She still fed Barbara every morning, but for the rest of the day she had had to be weaned. The grief of this mixed with all the other griefs, made her turn back into the house and sit at the table, letting her tears run out through her fingers. Their life before seemed dead and gone – as did the Ted she knew. And she was so changed herself: she with her terrible secret.

Even as she cried for all that was lost to all of them, she could not stop thinking about Johnny, the father of her child. It felt like a lifeline to think of him – as if he might now be the one way she had out of all this.

When it came down to it, she had not even seen Johnny many times. He worked shifts and lived over the other side of town, within reach of the main city fire station. It was winter, so it grew dark early and the weather was cold. When she thought back on it, they had only been together on fewer than a dozen occasions. And yet.

After that first night, warmed inside by the thin alcohol, but even more by his kisses, she had almost floated home from the bus stop in Ladywood, feeling somehow that she was in another world from her normal life. Walking home, she could hear the rumble and thump of the night shift going on in factories around her, the occasional muffled shout. But the night was calm. It had stopped snowing and the usually dark and mucky streets were silvered by snow and moonlight.

Nora was already in bed when she crept into the house. As Grace lay trying to sleep, the guilt rushed in on her.

What the hell was I playing at? Voices nagged in her head. But still her mind could not stop replaying the evening, excited by it. She just couldn't seem to think straight at all and decided it was the drink. It would all look different in the morning.

Next day at work, she carried out the repetitive tasks as music blared out and the girls around her sang along to the wireless. It was all right when they were jigging about to the 'Pistol Packin' Mama' but sooner or later it was 'I'll Be Seeing You'. The moment the emotional song began, she was thinking about all the familiar places she shared with Ted. But soon, even while she was thinking about the past, it was Johnny's face, Johnny's eyes, that kept stealing into her mind, fixed on her with that rapt attention and desire. Try as she might, she just could not stop thinking of him, and in her confusion and high emotion she burst into tears.

'Hey – what's up with you, Grace?' Margaret called, from her neighbouring work station. Her voice was half teasing, half concerned. 'I hope that fella you met last night ain't playing with your heart?'

This was far too near the truth. Grace wiped her eyes quickly.

'*No.* I'm just missing Ted, that's all. Going out last night brought it all back. I'd be best off not going.'

'Oh, don't talk so silly,' Margaret said. 'You don't have to live like a widow when you ain't one. Life's too short, kid.'

Had it not been for Margaret, Grace knew she might have retreated and never gone anywhere where she might meet Johnny Duke ever again. But of course, she did go. Not once, but again and again. Without a ring on her finger. And soon, he was all she could think about.

And now, once again, he seemed to be filling her mind.

Ted and Larry came in after a while, and though they had not been able to achieve anything much, she could see that trying to sort it out was good for Ted. His face was grey with exhaustion, but there was a lighter look to him and he managed to laugh and joke a bit with Larry.

They took chairs out to the back of the house, where there was a little blue-bricked area by the privy. Grace made tea. She was grateful to Larry for nattering away, even if all he talked about was pigeons. To say Larry was obsessed would be a bit of an understatement. A monologue followed on the various types of bird.

'What you wanna do is get some of them Rollers,' he said, leaning forward on his skinny thighs, a cigarette burning between the finger and thumb of his right hand.

'What are they, then?' Grace was still interested at this point.

'Oh!' He sat up. 'Beautiful, they are. And they was bred here, in Birmingham. Bloke called William Pensom. He was the greatest – a *genius*, 'e was. 'E were a bus driver – but 'e bred these birds that'd do backward rolls. They tumble' – his hands performed arcs in the sky – 'like little acrobats. It's a beautiful sight, that is. It *does* summat to yer.'

'Sounds lovely,' Grace said. And it did. Ted was sitting back, his painfully thin legs crossed one over the other, his clothes too big on him. But he was listening with interest.

However, by the time Larry had gone on about all the other sorts of pigeon Ted might consider – racers, tumblers and tipplers and fantails, on it went – and whether he could ever even get the wood for a decent coop and be here long enough to do anything about it – Grace was beginning to suffer from pigeon indigestion.

'How's Eileen?' she managed to get in at last, when Larry paused for breath.

'Oh . . .' He looked baffled for a second as if he had forgotten who Eileen was. 'Oh.' He grinned. 'Yeah – she's all right.'

Twelve

'Just give me a few more days,' Grace begged. She was sitting in Joan's kitchen, Barbara in her lap. On the table were the family's ration books and Joan's worn cloth bags, ready to go to the shops. Davey was scooting back and forth along the lino with a tin train.

Ted had been home a week and a half. Once again Grace was close to tears. She felt like a flaming tap these days, distressed and overwrought all the time.

'*Please*, Joan. I know it's a lot for you and Norm. But Ted's so . . .' She broke down then. 'He's so *different*. I'm at my wits' end. I can't get near him. He won't talk to me, won't go out. The slightest thing sets him off – makes him jump out of his skin. He just shouts . . .' She tried to pull herself together and looked across into Joan's worried and reproachful eyes.

'The only thing keeping him going – and me, for that matter – is Larry and that rotten old pigeon coop. He managed to get some old packing boxes to start mending the thing. It looks a terrible mess but it's keeping them both occupied.'

She drifted off and looked down at Barbara. 'You're a little darlin',' she said, awash with tenderness. But the thought she kept to herself, looking at her daughter's pale, plump cheeks and blonde hair, was, *She looks more and more like her daddy . . .* A blush, half shame, half longing, made its way from her neck to her face and all over, until she was sure it must be obvious to her sister. Luckily Joan, a pinner over her frock, was leaning down, ferreting through her cupboards, hoping, as they all did in the same way, that there might just be some extra thing to eat in there which they had forgotten – a tin, a handful of ancient raisins . . .

'Norm's not very happy about it all,' she said, head half in the low cupboard. Which, Grace knew, meant that *she* wasn't. Which Grace already knew. These days Joan was expressing disapproval in every line of her body.

'I'll do it. But just a few more days, that's all. Please, sis.'

As she said it, Davey banged his head on the table as he trotted past and started to howl. Joan tutted, standing upright again and lumbering over to Davey. How Joan managed to stay plump when there was so little to eat was a mystery to Grace, who was as thin as a rail. Though even Joan was not quite as big as she had once been.

'What difference is a few days going to make, that's what I want to know,' she said over Davey's yowls. She rubbed his head. 'You're all right, Davey – it were that table – just came up and hit you, daint it? Bad table!' She pretended to smack it and Davey gave a watery smile. 'Look, Grace – you got yourself into this mess. You've got to sort yourself out. You've got a husband and a child by another man . . .'

'Well, you're quick off the mark,' Grace snapped, getting to her feet with Barbara cuddled in her arms. 'Did you think I hadn't noticed or summat?'

Joan put her hands on her hips. 'I'll give you a few more days. But by God, Grace – you'd better tell him by then or I'll be round with her to tell him myself.'

'You wouldn't!' Grace was horrified. 'Don't you flaming dare!'

'Only if that's what it takes to make you see sense,' Joan said. She looked as if she was about to say something else.

Grace thought, if she says, *I never thought you were that kind of woman* again I swear I'll lamp her one . . . There had been a lot of that when she first had to confide to Joan that she had a baby on the way. *What sort of woman is that?* she'd retorted, burning with shame, knowing everyone would think she was *just* that sort of woman.

She handed Barbara over to Joan. Barbara gave a chirrup of laughter and Joan, in spite of herself, smiled down into her little niece's face.

'It's a good job you're such a cracker,' she said fondly.

Grace hurried to the shops for something – anything – to justify her morning trip out of the house. Her feelings were in turmoil, as ever. She thought of all the things she had not said to her sister: how the only time she and Ted could be close was when he wanted her in bed, in the dark, scarcely talking to her before or after. And how she wanted to love him with all her heart but he felt a million miles away. And how she couldn't get out of her head the feel of . . . *him* . . . The memory of him, his eyes on hers, his lovemaking. Until she thought she would go mad.

Thirteen

She never meant to go with Johnny Duke, not *like that*. If anyone had warned her when she and Johnny first met that this was where it would lead, that she would be unfaithful to Ted, she would have been shocked to the core. She wasn't *that kind of woman* – of course she wasn't. It was all just a bit of fun and company.

But never in her life before had she felt the way she did during those weeks in the spring of 1944. She and Johnny had been out for a drink here and there, snatched times in between work shifts, made harder by the blackout and Johnny working some distance away. It all made it easier to tell herself that this was nothing. He was just a man she had met, good for a chat in the pub now and then to lighten the boredom and dark days.

Except that she just could not stop thinking about him. When they met, they laughed a lot together. Johnny would tell her his next day off and they would meet in town, in one pub or another. She would tell Nora she was off out, and Nora was busy with her boyfriend by then. But she didn't mention it to Margaret and the others in the factory. And that, she thought now, was where it began – the way she learned to hide things and fib about it, even to herself. Especially to herself.

She lived for the moment, never asking herself what she thought she was doing on these nights when she and Johnny lingered together in a town pub, talking about their lives and families, about where they came from. Except that Grace never mentioned that she was married to a man called Ted who she had now not set eyes on for more than four years.

She felt as if she was in another life with Johnny, separate from her life with Ted. She was not really doing anything wrong.

The snow melted and spring arrived. And during those still shadowy evenings, she chose not to ask herself what she was doing lingering late in some shop doorway in New Street or in the shadow of the cathedral, she and Johnny in each other's arms. They were in a world of their own, kissing as if it was the most natural thing she had ever done.

The first time *it* happened (that was how she remembered it to herself) was in April. They had gone back to Steven's Bar. Among the crush in the bar were other lads from the fire station, regular firemen, along with a few AFS volunteers. None of Grace's pals from work were there. They did not know she was there either.

As it got to nine o'clock the others were drifting away. It was dark outside. Grace was leaning up against Johnny's shoulder, desperately not wanting to leave.

'I'll have to go,' she said reluctantly.

Johnny took her hand and squeezed it. 'Don't go yet, Grace.'

Their eyes met and what she saw in his made her look away, blushing. He had such a frank face, his eyes intense with longing. She found him irresistible.

'I don't want to – but I mustn't stop too late.' She knew that by the time they had lingered a while outside, it would be *much* later.

'All right, then.' Johnny downed his last mouthful of ale, making a comical face. 'Ugh.'

'I don't know why we do it to ourselves,' she said. They both laughed.

'Tell you what,' he said, standing up. 'I'll walk you home.'

'Walk?' she said, laughing. 'What – to Ladywood? But then you'll have to come all the way back.'

He shrugged his broad shoulders. 'So? I can walk fast.'

They walked along New Street in the chilly evening, Johnny's arm about her shoulders, hers round his waist. They fitted together so well, were just the right build for each other. The air smelt smoky and damp. Grace was grateful for the white-painted edges of the pavements. Johnny had a tiny torch which he turned on now and then, throwing down a thin streak of light.

'I still keep expecting to hear the air-raid warning go off any minute,' she said. It still went off now and then these days, but rarely.

'Yeah, I know.' He was silent for a moment. 'I've been down here a few bad nights, I can tell you. All ablaze – God, the heat. And the smoke! You could hardly see your hand in front of your face.'

There had been so much damage to the city. Survivors like the Times Furnishings building loomed at the far end of the High Street, but close to it, the corner of New Street and High Street had been torn away and all along New Street were jagged wounds of bomb damage.

She felt a shudder pass through his body and it made her feel tender towards him.

'It must have been so frightening,' she said. 'It was bad enough in the shelter, without being out in it.' They had spent so many cold, sleepless nights in the shelter in the back lane at Inkerman Street.

'Yeah,' he said. 'It was. But having to sit tight, hearing it all going on – well, that'd tear my nerves to shreds even worse. If you're up and doing you don't think too much. But then . . .'

He stopped, abruptly. Grace gave his waist a small squeeze. 'What?'

'Oh—' He forced a lighter tone. 'Just – a mate of mine, one of them nights . . . It was so hot you could feel it beating on yer . . . A beam came down on him. I saw him go down – in the flames. Couldn't do a thing. Still feel I should've done, though.'

She gasped, hearing him struggling with his voice, trying not to break down.

'Oh, Johnny – how terrible.'

'Yeah.' He gave a shrug. 'That's fighting fires. Anyhow, we was forty-eight hours on, bloody long shifts. But in between, sometimes they took us out to the country – to farms. We used to help out, like.'

'Did you, now?' she said, teasingly. She wanted to lighten things. They were leaving the city behind, winding their way into Ladywood. 'I s'pose you met some of those Land Girls?'

Johnny laughed. 'Oh yeah – we saw a few of them all right.'

'I could've done that, I s'pose,' she said. 'I just stayed in a factory – I daint want to go far from home. I don't know the first thing about the country and farming.'

'Nor did some of them,' Johnny said, chuckling. 'They had to learn fast, I can tell yer. Some of them were right townies. They was better off for grub out there, though – eggs and chickens and that. There was one lass, come out from Smethwick, used to send her mother a rabbit home in the post every week.'

'What – a live one?'

'No, yer daft bint – a dead'un. For Sunday dinner. Just

put a bit of paper round it with the address on, and off it went.'

'You're kidding?'

'I'm not! You can post anything if you've got the address on it! Eh you . . .' His voice changed, taking on an amorous warmth. He pulled her aside. The buildings were huddled either side of them, even darker shadows in the deepening night. Johnny switched on his torch. They were standing beside the wreckage of a house. 'Come on,' he hissed. 'Looks all right in here.'

'No!' Grace tried to pull him back. 'We can't go in there. It's dangerous – summat might come down on us.' She shivered, superstitious about bombed out houses 'You don't know what might be in there.'

'I'll have a look.' Johnny stepped inside and she saw the little pencil of light moving. 'Roof's already gone,' he reported in a loud whisper. 'There's nowt much left.'

'You sure there's no one in there?'

'No – come *on*.'

She stepped into the shell of a building, into its old stinks of wet, burned stuff and damp masonry. Everything felt unreal, like watching herself from the outside: a woman stepping into the darkness, into the arms of a man who was not her husband; a woman who was full of desire, who could not stop herself. Because she knew that once she was in there, his arms would be waiting.

'That's it,' he said, drawing her to him.

At last, all she had been waiting for, the comfort and excitement of his arms around her. She was not thinking, not intending, just needing. They pressed each other close in the darkness, his hands moving on her body, hers drawing him against her until they could not stop, could not draw back.

All they had was their two coats, which they laid on

the floor, hurrying, taking off only what was necessary, both in a fever of need so that suddenly Johnny was on top of her, a vigorous man full of energy and desire. Her back was pressed against the brick floor through only a layer of cloth, but whatever the discomfort, she was too carried away to care.

They clung to one another and Grace found herself sobbing as Johnny kissed her again and said, 'Oh God, Gracie, you're lovely, you're my girl.' Full of the bliss of release, of being held, she kept repeating his name, warmed by his body, her hands stroking his strong back. It was only as they cooled and came back to themselves that she started to feel the pain of the hard floor against her spine.

He walked her home afterwards, the two of them wrapped together, stopping every few yards to kiss. She stopped him some distance from Inkerman Street to say goodbye. She wasn't taking any chances of anyone seeing her, even at this time of night. She had told him she lived with her mother, who was a tartar.

It happened just once more, a fortnight later, in the same place. She had not seen him at all during those days and by the time they met she was longing for him, to be held and loved again. When he offered to walk her home again, they both knew what was going to happen. Neither of them said anything. Grace felt that if she spoke, it would bring reality crashing in on them. Her silence meant she was not lying, to him, to herself. It was like a beautiful dream that they shared, just the two of them, away from the war, from everything.

'When will I see you again?' she asked as he left her at the corner again. She felt warm and happy after their lovemaking.

'I'm off next Thursday, I think,' he said. 'Grace—' She

could sense, in the darkness, that he was looking at her very seriously. 'I don't want to let you go. I mean, don't think this is just . . . I'm not playing about. I want to be your man. Why don't we go and see your mom – get wed, like?'

Grace plummeted to earth with a crash. Panic seized her. How the hell could she have let this happen, let this man think that she was free and available?

'Oh – Johnny,' she said, desperately searching for words to let him down lightly. 'Not now – it's late. Mom'll be asleep. She won't thank us for waking her up! Look . . . Let's just keep things as they are, for now, eh? What with the war on and everything. I don't know as I'm ready to get settled yet . . .'

'But I thought . . .' She could feel the disappointment coming from him. He sounded surly with hurt. 'I love you, Grace. I do. I ain't mucking about.'

'Oh, Johnny – I love you too,' she said, throwing her arms round him, wanting to say something to make him feel better. 'I do! Only let's not rush anything, eh? It's just, the war – anything can happen. Like you said about your mate who was killed in the fire. I couldn't bear it if something happened to you.'

'All right,' he said, seeming to accept this. 'But you're my girl, right?'

'Course I am.' She kissed him. 'Goodnight, love – I'd better go.'

'I love you,' she heard him say as they moved away from each other.

When they parted that night, it was the last time she ever saw him.

The next Thursday evening, she went to where they said they would meet, by the cathedral. Grace waited and waited. She had been wondering what she should say, torn apart by knowing she should tell him the truth. She could not keep stringing Johnny along. He was a decent man with real feelings for her. She knew she had done a terrible thing – both to him and to Ted. That night she stood by the wall of St Philip's, cold with dread. The thought of losing him was unbearable. But she had done him wrong – she knew she had to tell him.

He never came. She waited and waited in the dark before dragging her way home, hurt and confused. She told herself that they must have had a change of work rota. But how could he get in touch with her now? She had never let him know her address. Days passed. Two weeks. She waited, sick with loss and worry.

Only well into May 1944 did one of her workmates who knew some of the firemen tell her that a group of them had been posted away, down south. Later, after June, and the invasions on D-Day, it all fell into place. They had been needed for something down there. He had not left her without a single word after all.

But she had no idea where he was. And soon after that, she started to feel strange. She was never actually sick when she was carrying Barbara, but she did feel odd. Her appetite changed and she had a nasty taste in her mouth. One day she passed out at work. It had barely crossed her mind that she would catch for a baby. It had never happened with Ted. Babies were not for her, she had thought. It took her a while to realize what was happening.

As the summer passed, and as her body began to swell and she felt movements inside her, it gradually dawned on her. She was not barren after all! She was going to have a baby. And what's more, a baby that was nothing to do with her husband – something that was going to be perfectly obvious to everyone.

Fourteen

When she got back to the house from Joan's that morning, Grace pushed open the back door to find Ted asleep in the chair in the kitchen. He did not stir even when she opened and closed the door.

Grace crept to the table, put her bag down and went over to look at him. Ted was very still, his mouth slightly open, and for a second her heart sped in panic. She heard him let out a small breath and her pulse slowed again.

As she stood looking at him, she was filled with shame and desperation. Ted's jaw looked longer now he was so thin. He had caught a touch of sun out in the garden with Larry, but he still looked sallow and unhealthy. The old Ted would never have fallen asleep at this time in the morning. He sagged in the chair like an old man.

What has happened to you? she thought, gazing down at him. She had to remind herself, *He's my husband.*

She crept over and put the kettle on the gas. Bending over the waste bucket, she knocked the old grouts out of the teapot – *SWAN BRAND*, she read, stamped on the bottom . . . And a memory of Johnny came to her, so powerful that it set her heart thudding again . . . Walking along in the dark with him, their arms around each other, his kiss on her cheek. Johnny, who now seemed to be working just around the corner.

Oh God, she thought, turning to look at Ted again, this

strange, broken man in the room with her. I've got to stop this. I've got to try and understand him, be kind to him.

In the daytime Ted never did anything much until Larry visited after work. He seemed completely exhausted. He would go outside and stand for long periods, a cigarette burning in his hand. Then he would come back in and just sit. He never even read the paper.

'He's bad, in't 'e?' Larry had said to her a couple of times, his boyish, freckly face looking troubled. 'I thought 'e might perk up a bit quicker than this.'

'I know,' Grace agreed. Hearing this only made her feel more desperate. 'But you coming round's a big help, Larry.'

'Is it?' he said, mouth turning down despondently. 'It's hard to tell, to be honest with yer. 'E barely says a word.'

She reassured him that it was a help. She knew Ted was silent and impossible to read. It was only at night that he wasn't quiet, when the restless lashing out and talking began. She would wake, her heart banging, as Ted muttered or bawled things, enraged-sounding scraps of words that he never seemed to remember the next morning. At night, in the dark bedroom, she was frightened of him.

It certainly was a help to have Larry take Ted off her hands for a part of the day. Because that was how it felt – as if he was a heavy weight, loaded on top of her, leaving her deprived of her beloved little girl and with no room to breathe.

Larry arrived later on, carrying in each hand a plank with nails sticking out at each end. Grace stood at the back door in the warm afternoon, arms folded, leaning into the door frame. Once the two men were absorbed, measuring up, banging and sawing, she went upstairs.

When Ted came home, he had thrown his bag into the cupboard in their room. Later he had produced a couple of things out of it that needed washing, but otherwise, there it had sat. Now she thought, *I'll just have a little look inside, in case* – she pretended to herself – *there's anything else needs washing.*

She had no real idea what soldiers carried about with them. And somewhere in her mind, as she went to the cupboard, feeling horribly nervous, she knew she was looking for clues. To what? Clues that would tell her who was this man, her husband? Letters, from someone other than herself? A photograph, perhaps, given to him by some sweetheart over there he was still pining for, some Polish woman? She realized she could hardly imagine what a Polish woman would look like – blonde, dark? Nothing about Ted's life over the past five years was known to her.

The cupboard opened with a squeak and the mucky canvas bag lay flat at the bottom. She could see immediately that there was nothing much inside, if anything at all. Somehow disappointed, she picked it up. It smelt strongly, but of nothing in particular, just a stink of stored-up grime. But there was something in there: a weight heavier than the bag.

Unfastening the straps, she reached inside and pulled out a little sewing kit, wrapped in grubby white cloth. *Hussif* – she remembered what the soldiers called it. And there was something else – a roll of paper wrapped in a scrap of black rag. Her breath caught. Letters? It did not look like *her* letters, her cheerful attempts to keep up the thread between them. Where had they gone? she wondered.

Jumping at a sound from somewhere, she ran into the back room and checked where Ted and Larry were, but they were both still busy outside.

Back in their bedroom, she fumbled to untie the knot in the rag, cursing her trembling fingers. Her blood was running fast. There was dread at what she might find – and a kind of excitement. Ted had secrets too. Was this thing that he had hidden in here something to make him equal with her? Could she feel the weight of guilt lift from her or at least be balanced with some guilt on his side?

The papers were thin, lined stuff, torn from a cheap pad. It all kept trying to roll back up again as she opened it out. On each sheet was a drawing of a bird. She did not know about birds, but she could see that they were good drawings, beautiful drawings, done with a pencil. Whose were they? She frowned, looking at them. And why was Ted carrying them about with him? She was not sure if she was more relieved or disappointed. It just made him seem even further away from her.

She quickly rolled them back up and retied the strip of rag, desperately not wanting to be caught snooping in his things. Once she had returned the bag to the cupboard, she checked through the back window again. All safe. They were still out there.

Soberly, with a sense of desperate bewilderment, she went back down to make the men a cuppa.

When she and Ted got into bed that night, she was determined that they would not just lie in the dark in silence again. The longer Ted was at home, the harder it became to know where to start with asking him about anything. She knew so little that she hardly knew what to ask. She pulled the bedclothes over the two of them, feeling shivery and nervous.

'Ted?' She made herself speak. Her voice came out high and forced.

'Yeah?' He was already lying down, on his back. He spoke cautiously, as if expecting trouble or difficulty. It was not a welcoming response. Trying not to cry or make him feel any worse, she lay down beside him.

'Love . . .' Timidly, she laid a hand on his ribs and felt him flinch. How thin he was. It shocked her every time she touched him. 'You feel so far away,' she pleaded. 'Can't you talk to me a bit? Tell me what happened, or . . .' She trailed off, already discouraged. *Why have you got drawings of birds in your bag?* She really didn't know if this meant anything or not, other than that he had not shown them to her.

He lay still for a moment and she wondered what he was thinking and whether he would start talking. She felt his arm twitch beside her.

'I just wanted to ask . . .' she tried. Taking courage, she tried a different approach. 'I – I wasn't being nosy . . . I thought you might have some washing . . .' As she began, she saw how impossible this was to say. *I looked through your bag. I unwrapped your papers and looked at them, your drawings . . .*

And he wasn't listening anyway, was turning away from her, onto his side. 'Don't keep on, woman,' he said. 'Let's get some sleep.'

Her hand slid from him as he turned away and she was left lying beside his scrawny back, the back she used to know like a map of home. The back of someone who used to tell her she was beautiful, the most gorgeous girl in all the world. Someone who had loved her. Where had he gone now?

Ted fell asleep quickly. He seemed steeped in exhaustion.

Grace lay feeling her blood pounding around her body. She knew she was not going to sleep and eventually, as

Ted's breathing turned to a jagged snoring, she slipped out of bed, pulled a jersey on over her nightdress and went downstairs. She tucked herself up in the chair in the kitchen, the rug over her knees.

Her thoughts piled one on another. She longed for Barbara, asleep over in Joan's house. The thought of her baby brought on an aching milk reflex. Tears filled her eyes and she got up to fetch a rag to dry herself. She could see no way out of this . . . This wounded stranger upstairs, the loss of her child . . .

Except that in a month or so, Ted was due to go back to the army, to be sent into active duty again. Surely he was in no state? And yet – terrible thoughts came to her – they would make him go, and then who knew if he would ever return? She would be alone again. And all this time, so near, doing his bit in the fire service, the father of her child . . .

Grace pulled her knees up close, resting her head on them and rocking gently back and forth, trying to comfort herself. She gave herself over to thinking about Johnny: his cheerful personality, his eagerness for her, his vigorous body as he had given her love, given her the thing she had thought she would never have – a child, her lovely Barbara. Their Barbara.

I'm no good to Ted, she thought, as her tears flowed, silver drops on the rug. *He doesn't want me. Not really. He's not the man I married any more. I don't even know who he is.* She laid her head sideways on her knees, trying to force the train of her thoughts to stop, but they would not obey.

Don't I owe it to Johnny, and to Barbara, to see him and tell him? Johnny had not just gone off and left her, as she had feared when he did not turn up that night. He had been posted far away and had no way of getting in touch

78

with her anyway. The war had separated them, as it had separated herself and Ted. But she and Johnny had a child together. This thought obsessed her. Ted did not seem to want her – he was a million miles away. Maybe Ted would prefer her just to let him go. Was it really Johnny she should be with?

Fifteen

She could think of almost nothing else. Moving around her silent stranger of a husband, she burned with longing for her little girl, for all that was familiar. Even though she had not seen Johnny for almost a year, she felt closer to him than she did to Ted. And all the time she knew her chances were running out. She had to tell Ted about Barbara, or Joan and Norm would be coming round with her – that's if one of the neighbours didn't get there first.

It was less difficult to get out of the house to see Barbara on these mornings now. Ted never asked her where she was going. He was so wrapped up in himself that he didn't seem to care. He had only been back to see his own mother and father once more and apart from that the only person he bothered with was Larry. He had been to see Larry's birds a few times, as Larry only lived a couple of streets away.

'By the weekend, Grace,' Joan said again that Wednesday morning. 'I've had enough.'

Grace let her hair fall forward to hide her face as she looked down at Barbara, who was suckling while waving one arm in the air. She seemed a bit snuffly and Grace was immediately worried. Was she getting a cold – perhaps becoming really sick?

'All right,' she agreed. What else could she say? Studying Barbara, all she could see was Johnny, his eyes, his colouring. Johnny, the father of her child.

By the weekend, she would have done the deed. Then none of it would matter anyway. A helpless feeling of fate had come over her ever since she had first thought of going to find Johnny. I'm damned if I do and damned if I don't, she thought.

'There, you little monkey,' she said to Barbara, lifting her to change sides. She was trying to sound normal, as if everything in her life did not make her feel she was on the surge of a great river, carrying her over a waterfall in which she had no idea if she would drown.

At first, the idea of going to find Johnny had been just a fancy, a dream. But now it possessed her thoughts completely. She had argued herself into thinking it was the proper thing to do. Johnny had a right, she told herself. *And Ted – Ted acts as if I'm like the ball and chain they joke about when you get married. Only now, it feels real.*

All day she fretted. Her body was electric with nerves, her pulse constantly running too fast, as if she was poised to run away. By that afternoon, after she had cooked Ted some dinner, once again he was asleep in the chair. She stood looking at him, full of desperation. She had loved him once, with all her heart. She was trying so hard to love him now, but nothing she did ever seemed to be right. He rejected all her attempts to be close. He did not love her, beyond wanting her body – sometimes. And, she realized now, it was not she who could not have children. It was as if he had withheld this from her too. Everything was a fog of confusion and sadness.

All she could think of now was Johnny. She could not help herself. As if it was some other woman who, while Ted was out at the back later with Larry, slipped silently out of the front door. A woman in her old summer frock with pink roses on it, her hair pinned back prettily, lying black and glossy on her shoulders. Whose feet, in her little black shoes, took her along Monument Road towards where she had caught sight of Johnny before, as if in repeating the walk she might see him in exactly the same spot.

But of course he was not there.

For a few seconds she was at a loss. But those feet took her onwards, towards the fire station. She stopped just short of it, suddenly feeling foolish. *What the hell am I doing here?* she thought. Goose pimples rose on her skin. *I'm married – to Ted. What am I doing?* She struggled to take a deep breath. She could not stop, could not just move away. But nor could she manage to go and knock on the door . . .

For a few minutes she paced up and down the road. However long it took, she *had* to stay there. Sooner or later she would see him, she knew. She *had* to see him. As she turned back towards the fire station, her blood thudded harder at the sight of a man in a fireman's uniform coming along the road from the other direction. At once she could see that it was not Johnny. The man was dark-haired, tall, walking with a loping stride.

They coincided more or less outside the station. ''Scuse me—' She tried to sound casual. 'Is there a bloke called Johnny Duke working in there?'

She waited for the man's eyes to take on a suggestive look, as some men's would have done. But he was a gangling, innocent-looking lad.

'Yeah,' he said. 'D'yer wanna speak to him?'

'If that's all right,' she said.

In the moments it took for him to lope into the station and find Johnny, she could have changed her mind, could have run away. But she stood with her hands folded in front of her, past caring if anyone thought her strange. It felt as if fate had taken hold of her. She could not move.

A fireman with blond hair and a muscular, easy stride came out of the station. In that second Grace realized she and Johnny had never seen each other in full daylight before. But she knew him straight away, that walk, that body.

He paused, puzzled; saw her. His pace quickened, a smile breaking out across his face.

'Is that you, Gracie?' He laughed, and suddenly he was there in front of her. He was a little smaller than she remembered, but the easy smile was just the same, his blue eyes direct as he looked down at her. 'Fancy seeing you!'

'Well, I only live down the road, don't I?' she said, with a pang that he didn't seem to remember this.

'Oh ah – I know.' He pushed his hands down into his pockets and gazed at her, affectionately, she thought. 'But I never exactly knew where you was – you never told me!'

But, her mind thought, insecurely, if you had really tried to find out . . . She wanted to begin, to tell him. But he was so casual, so much part of another time, somehow, that she did not know how to start.

'In fact,' he went on, looking at her with what seemed to be half-joking reproach, 'you never told us quite a few things, did yer?'

'What d'you mean?' Dread fixed like a cold stone in the back of her throat.

'Well – it was one of your pals from the factory told me you was married.'

Grace stared back at him. She felt blood pour into her face, a mortified burning in her cheeks. Johnny's eyes were harder now, accusing. Under his gaze she felt cheap and terribly ashamed. She looked down, at the ground, at his heavy boots.

'Who – Margaret?' she managed to say.

'I dunno,' he said easily. 'Can't remember 'er name.'

She dared to look back at him again.

'You should've told me, Grace.' He looked sad now, which was much worse. 'I was sweet on you – I thought . . .'

'I'm sorry.' She managed to say it through the lump in her throat, trying to force back her tears.

'Well, they sent us away after that.' Johnny shrugged. 'Down to Southampton, so I thought, well, that's for the best. Anyhow . . .' He shifted his weight from one foot to the other, looked down, then back at her, seeming bashful. 'Turned out all right. I'm getting wed – next month. Moving away. Susan's coming back up to Leek with me – we want a quieter life than here.'

'Oh.' Grace summoned all her pride and forced her face into a smile. 'That's really nice news, Johnny. Good for you. I hope you'll both be very happy.' She gathered herself. 'Anyroad, I'd best be moving on.'

He frowned. 'How d'you know I was here, anyway?'

'Saw you, the other day.' She kept up the smile, talking for all the world as if none of it mattered, as if it was nothing. 'I just thought I'd come and say hello.'

Johnny looked at her seriously for a second, as if about to say something. Her heart quickened. In the end he said, 'You're looking fine.' He was backing away now. 'Nice to see yer, Grace – all the best.'

'Bye, Johnny,' she said, struggling to steady her voice.

He had already turned and was walking away. She stood watching, unable to move, actually hearing in her mind, as if it was real, a door slamming, a great heavy oak thing closing with a doom-laden boom.

At last she moved away, cold even in the sunshine. Raising her chin, she gathered herself to walk home.

There was only one thing she could do now. And then she would have to take the consequences.

When she tiptoed back into the house, Ted and Larry were still absorbed only yards away at the end of the garden. Grace stood in her back room, trying to slow her breathing. To her astonishment she realized she had been out for barely half an hour. And in that time it felt as if she had lived years' worth of life and everything had shifted without anyone around her noticing.

III

Sixteen

I've got to tell him.

Grace hardly slept that night. The nights were disturbed in any case by Ted's restlessness. This time he did not shout or sit up, but every so often, just as she was tilting into sleep, he would begin twitching and muttering and she was forced wide awake again.

She lay on her back, her thoughts swirling. In the darkness everything looked its worst. Everything was coming home to roost. She had done a wicked thing. The moment of hurt she had seen in Johnny's eyes was magnified now. She had deceived two men, and was now going to hurt them both. She had behaved like a hussy, and now she deserved any punishment that came to her.

Looking back from a distance now on those winter days when she could think of nothing but Johnny Duke, she was amazed and disgusted. All that overwhelming longing she had felt for him – to be held and made love to. What kind of woman was she?

She turned over onto her side, away from Ted. What on earth was this wrecked, angry man going to do when she told him? Anything could happen. He might kill her! Or he might go completely to pieces. The blood was beating so fast in her body that she was unable to lie still any longer. She got up and went downstairs again.

Sitting in the kitchen, she hatched a desperate plan. She would fetch Barbara from Joan's tomorrow and take her away. Just leave and go somewhere where they would both be safe. She imagined herself with Barbara in one arm, getting onto the tram, then a train, to . . . Where?

Where the hell d'you think you're going to go? she whispered. *We've no one else in the world.* The thought of leaving Joan behind was desolate. Ever since they were children, she had relied on Joan. Her sister was like a pillar, holding up her life.

And what would she live on if Ted was to throw her out? She could get a job, but then who would have Barbara?

And so, all night, her thoughts ran back and forth. She met the dawn exhausted and overwrought.

I'll tell him this morning, she thought, as the light seeped into the room. She got stiffly to her feet to boil water. *I'll go up now and tell him.*

Ted was still asleep when she went up with two mugs of weak tea. She stood looking down at him, at his cropped hair, his thin face, the brows pulled into a frown even in his sleep. So pure and good, my Ted, she thought. Never done a thing wrong in his life. He could never understand.

Gently, she put his tea down and climbed in again on her side of the bed. And when he woke, and sat up to drink his tea, giving her, to her surprise, a brief, sleepy smile, still she could not say a word. Both of them seemed to be locked in, with no way out.

Thursday passed, much like the other days. Grace was finding it hard to eat anything, she was so churned up. Every time there was a moment when she thought she might sit down by her husband and try to begin, she would turn and look at him and imagine herself saying, 'Ted – there's something I need to tell you . . .' But it was impossible.

Tonight, she told herself. *We'll go to bed and I'll hold him in my arms. Tell him like that. I can't do it sitting here in the kitchen.*

By five o'clock she stood barefoot in the kitchen, going through the motions of cooking tea: a pan of butter beans, a few shreds of meat. Ted was outside: not with Larry this time, just pottering about down the end.

Well, Grace thought, peering at the pale concoction in the pan, *I just hope this lot tastes better than it looks.* Not that she really cared. She wasn't hungry anyway.

As she put the lid back on the saucepan, she heard a knock at the front door and her heart began to slam like a piston. Joan! And Norm! Joan had said she wouldn't come, not today, maybe not until Sunday, but maybe for some reason she had changed her mind and this was the moment Ted was going to be confronted with Barbara.

'Oh God, oh God, no, please . . .' she was muttering, creeping into the front room to peer out. She hardly dared look, fearing to see her sister's figure looming on the doorstep with Barbara in her arms.

Instead, on the pavement was a very thin, pale young man with short brown hair and a neat-looking brown jacket. Who, Grace thought, must have the wrong house. She rushed to the back to slip her shoes on.

'Yes?' She hoped she didn't seem too strange to him as she opened the door. Her heart rate was only just beginning to slow towards normal.

'Oh, er, hello.' He seemed shy and nicely spoken. And startled by the sight of her. 'I'm looking for a man called Ted Chapman. Is this the right house?'

'Yes,' she said warily. Had they come to take him back to the army, was her first thought. But wasn't it redcaps, who came? 'Who is it wants him?'

'Nothing to worry about, Mrs, er . . . Chapman?' he

guessed, with a faint smile. She saw he had a sweet, kindly face, but that he was painfully thin. 'I'm Kenneth Allen – I was with your husband in the . . . in Poland. I'm passing through Birmingham and I thought I'd just see how he's getting on.'

Grace led him through to the back, relieved. The young man seemed very nice. And it might do Ted good to see someone.

'He's out there.' She pointed through the back window. 'He's trying to fix up the pigeon coop.'

Kenneth leaned towards the window, narrowing his eyes. Ted was standing with his back to them, hands on his hips, a thin pole of a man, apparently staring at his handiwork.

'How is he getting on, Mrs Chapman?' Kenneth asked her, stepping back again. She could hear great concern in his voice and she turned to look at him, unsure what to say to this polite stranger, who nevertheless perhaps knew her husband much better than she did these days.

As she hesitated, Kenneth Allen seemed to see something in her eyes. His expression was very serious.

'I don't know if you know just how lucky Ted is to be alive,' he said.

'No.' Grace's voice was husky. 'Not – really. I can see he's not been well.'

As Kenneth began to speak, Ted turned and started to walk towards the house. Kenneth gently took Grace's arm and guided her back from the window.

'He wasn't in a good way when we left the camp – Stalag XXB. Some of us had to carry him at the end. Between us. We never thought he would make it this far.'

He saw her shocked expression.

'Has he not told you?'

'Nothing,' she whispered. She felt hopeless, as if she

was the one who had failed him. 'I mean – nothing about the camp, about what happened – how you got back.'

'We walked, like I said.' He spoke quickly and very quietly. 'From January. Through Germany. It was more than two months before we ran into the Yanks. Quite a few didn't make it . . .' With a shadow of a smile, he said. 'Ted must have survived to see his lovely wife again.'

They could hear his footsteps on the bricks outside the back door. Kenneth gave her a meaningful look and stepped away from her.

Ted stopped in the doorway and they turned to him. He stood quite still, a haunted expression on his face.

'Hello, Ted, old pal,' Kenneth said, going towards him.

Grace twisted inside as she saw her husband's face contort. He held out his arms to Kenneth Allen and fell upon him, sobbing like a child.

Seventeen

Grace shyly asked Kenneth if he would like to stay and have tea with them, though wishing to goodness she had something better to offer than her butter bean mess.

'No thanks, Mrs Chapman,' he said, to her relief. 'It's good of you but I'm on the way to Shrewsbury to see my grandfather. He's expecting me later tonight. I mustn't stop for long.'

She had told Ted to take Kenneth into the front room while she at least made him a cup of tea. She was very grateful to Kenneth for coming, for Ted having some company.

When she carried the tea in, the two men were talking quietly. Ted seemed to have recovered himself but he still looked haunted and emotional. Grace was filled with a wash of tenderness for him. It was the affectionate tone in which Kenneth Allen had talked about Ted, the concerned way he had looked at her. *My husband*, she thought, watching the two of them. After the turmoil and pain of yesterday, suddenly she felt able to turn all her feelings towards him, as if Kenneth's arrival had shifted something in her. She was the one in the wrong. Johnny was nothing in her life. That was gone. She must look after her poor Ted with all her heart.

'Thanks, Mrs Chapman.' Kenneth turned to her, smiling. 'I'm sorry for turning up with no warning. I've come from Warwick and it was a bit of a last-minute decision.'

'Don't be silly,' she told him. 'It's ever so nice of you to've come. Isn't it, Ted?'

Ted gave a wan smile but she had already seen what it meant to him. And it was such a relief to have someone else in the house for a while, someone who understood things that she didn't understand herself. She could see it had made a difference to Ted.

'Shame you can't stay longer,' she said. And meant it.

'You're not looking too bad, Ted, all things considered,' Kenneth said, a teasing note in his voice now.

And to Grace's surprise, Ted gave a laugh, though it had a bitter edge. He sat forward on his chair by the grate, elbows leaning on his long thighs.

'I s'pose he's shown you his marvellous drawings?' Kenneth said. 'What a talent! That was something you learned along the way, wasn't it, Ted?' He looked at Grace. 'Terribly boring, at times, those places. But this one, he was forever off – anything he could find to draw on or with . . .' He smiled. 'You ought to see about taking it up professionally, Ted.'

There was an awkward silence. Grace, amazed by this, saw Ted look at the floor, seeming embarrassed, but still wearing a faint smile.

'What did you do – before?' Grace asked Kenneth.

'In civvy street?' Kenneth said. 'Oh, carpentry. Restoring furniture, mainly. Always been better with my hands than my brain!'

Grace nodded, smiling. She liked Kenneth. Despite what he said, he seemed an intelligent, well-to-do person.

They chatted a little longer. While Grace was burning to ask a hundred questions – she wished she could have talked more to Kenneth on his own – she could tell that neither of them wanted to talk about the past. They stuck to light subjects of the present. Ted said he was seeing about keeping pigeons. Kenneth, like Ted, was on leave. He said he was playing a bit of cricket, though he ran out of energy easily. He was single and still living with his mother and father. As he stood up to go, Ted got up as well.

'Well, old mate,' Kenneth said, patting Ted on the back, 'I don't know if they'll call us up together again when the time comes. Who knows? Let's hope so, eh?'

Ted nodded vaguely, as if he could not even bear to talk about the idea of going back into the army.

'Look, I'll walk yer to the end of the road, mate. You've come all this way.'

'All right, then,' Kenneth said easily. He turned to Grace, holding out his hand. 'Very nice to meet you, Mrs Chapman. Thanks for the tea.'

'I'm glad you came,' she said sincerely. 'Come again – any time.'

As the two men went out, she thought how much better Kenneth looked than Ted. He was terribly thin as well, but he didn't seem anything like as ruined or emotional. For a moment she wanted to call after him, *Don't go – please don't leave us alone! Come back and tell me where my old husband has gone, because I don't know this one . . .*

But they were already halfway along the street. She turned the gas on again and got the table laid. When Ted did not come back after a few minutes, she went to the front to look. She jumped slightly at seeing him there, not far away, drifting slowly along the street with his head down.

Grace retreated into the house, feeling she was intruding on him. She waited in the kitchen, knotted up inside with nerves. *I am frightened because my husband is coming back into the house*, she thought. She was not afraid of anything he might do to her, but of the chasm of distance between them.

Ted came around the back. Once again, he hesitated in the doorway. Grace, standing at the stove, turned to face him. His face was working and she could see that he was quivering all over, seeming overwhelmed by emotion. Kenneth Allen's visit seemed to have unlocked something in him as well.

'Ted?' She spoke softly, scared, but stepping towards him. It was up to her, she thought, to move towards him. 'What is it, love?'

'I . . . You . . .' He stumbled into speech, beginning to weep again. 'You're so damn beautiful, Gracie. I can't . . . I've never been good enough for you. And now . . .' He couldn't finish, and shook his head, tears beginning to run down his cheeks.

'Ted – no, don't!' She went to him, tried to touch him, but he flung her off in his distress. His thinking these things seemed appalling in the light of what she had done, how she was the one in the wrong, who had betrayed him. She knew now, more than ever before, how much she longed for things to be right, for them just to love each other. 'Ted – please . . .'

He stormed across the room, pulled out a chair and sat forwards again, leaning on his thighs, but not still or settled. He swayed from side to side as the words jerked from him.

'For God's sake, Grace. I'm a mess. I can't . . . I don't . . .' He put his hands over his face for a moment.

She stood close, wanting to put a hand on his tensed shoulders, to try and break through to him, comfort him. But words were pouring out of him now from behind his hands.

'You've always been better than me. And now look at

me. I can't do anything. I can't even give yer a child – never could, could I? I'm no sort of man, not for a woman like you . . .'

He sat back so suddenly that she jumped. He looked up at her, his face shining with tears.

'You've got your life. You've managed without me all this time. I don't deserve you, Grace. I've nothing to give yer. Why don't you go – just leave me be and make yourself a life somewhere, eh? Why've you even waited for me? I'm no sort of husband for you . . .'

'No,' she protested. '*No*, Ted!' She was horrified by his words. All this time she knew that she was the villain, the one who had betrayed him – and here was her blameless, sick husband, bringing everything down upon himself. And after all her confusion over Johnny, just as she had come back to him, wanting to make everything better, he was blaming himself . . .

She flung herself down on her knees next to his chair. 'Please, love – don't . . . You're my husband. I love you, and I'm the one . . .' She gazed at him, willing the words to come out, but at that moment she could not do it to him. 'Don't say things like that,' she finished, sobbing. '*Please* don't.'

Ted looked down at her. 'Get up, Grace. Don't kneel by me.'

He took her hand and urged her up from the hard floor. Humbly she stood, looking down at him. Ted got to his feet and gently pushed her thick hair back from her shoulders. His eyes seemed to search hers and she trembled under his gaze. At least he was talking, talking about something, anything . . .

'I'm serious, Grace,' he said. 'Having Kenneth here – he's a good lad. Golden. Saved my life, he did – with one or two of the others. But when I saw you next to him I

98

thought, that's the kind of man she ought to be with. A proper man – who can give her a family, look after her proper, like . . .'

'But . . .' she began faintly. She found her knees were about to give way. *I must say it, now*, she urged herself. She had been given this moment, but it still felt so impossible. 'You're my husband,' she managed. 'I want you . . .'

'You've no future with me.' He looked desolate, but serious. He was no longer weeping. 'What've you got to look forward to? They'll send me away again. I might not come through this time. And even if I do . . .'

Their eyes were locked together. She felt as if he could see right into her, yet she knew also that he was innocent, that he would have no idea. She was shaking her head.

'Ted,' she said. 'I'm not good. I'm not what you think.' She could see his eyes disagreeing with her. Her legs were giving way. She pulled a chair to her and sank onto it, trembling all over.

'Please, Ted. Sit down. There's summat I've got to tell you.'

He brought the other chair and they sat side by side, like children in a classroom. She did not load him with details, but told him the bare truth. A little girl. Five months old. With Joan. The father did not matter. She would never see him again.

'It was all a terrible, terrible mistake,' she said. 'I don't know what happened to me. I just . . . It had been so long and I . . . I just wanted someone to put their arms around me . . .' Quietly, she sat weeping, feeling utterly wrung out. There. She had said it. Now she would have to take what came.

For a few moments she wondered if Ted had even heard what she said. He sat staring ahead of him. She could see that his hands were shaking, just as hers were.

She felt her whole being sway as if a powerful wind were blowing through the house.

'A daughter,' he said, to himself, not to her. Then turned and looked at her. His expression was intense, awful. 'You've got a daughter?' Grace nodded, her cheeks burning with shame.

He was on his feet. 'Well – you won't be needing me, then. Got everything you need, haven't yer?'

'Ted!'

But he was out through the back door.

'Don't – don't go!' She hurled herself after him, out along the entry, but he was far quicker than she was. By the time she got to the pavement he was well along the street, head down, his arms pumping feverishly as he marched away from her.

Eighteen

All she could do was wait. And wait.

All evening, there was never a moment when she was in any other state than waiting. Every fibre of her was primed, listening for him, worrying.

At first she thought he would just stop out for a while, trying to calm himself down before he came back. She had no idea where he might have gone and when he might come back. She could not eat, or sleep, or do anything else. She sat tensed, listening to every sound as darkness fell.

There was no question of her going to bed. She stayed in the chair, hair loose like a veil over her shoulders, pulling the rug over her as it grew cooler in the small hours of the next morning. All she could think about was Ted, the man she had married, who had been away all this time and lost himself. Who had come back a different man, or at least a shell of the man he had once been.

He had always been shy and quiet. They were so young when they first met, but once they had got to know each other again when they had both grown up a bit, she had loved his dry sense of humour. Ted would greet her with, 'All right, our kid?' and give a wink, mocking himself before his face broke into a shy grin. His eyes were always full of happiness at seeing her. Now she realized there had been a sense of amazement too, that a girl like her, with her dark, petite looks, her dancing blue eyes and lively personality, was interested in a shy boy like him. Her heart ached at the thought. Ted had never really seen past her looks and apparent confidence to realize how lost a girl she was, with no mom, no family except for Joan. Auntie Rose was dead and Grace hungry to belong, to have a family. Ted was a sweet, rock-like boy and she had clung to him. Despite everything, despite the war and their lack of children, which she had thought was her own fault anyway, she knew it had not been the wrong decision.

And now the war had broken so many things. The sodding war: those Germans wrecking everything, destroying lives. But – and this was the hardest thing to face – she had broken things just as much. She wept bitterly, remembering Johnny's face as she had last seen him. As well as hurt, his eyes had held contempt – and she knew she deserved it. A married woman, playing around, not telling him the truth. She had ruined everything.

But Barbara . . . She sobbed harder still. Despite all of it, she would never, ever want to be without her little girl, who was the joy of her life.

The clock struck two.

She sat on, all cried out for the moment, her ears pricked for any sound. Eventually, she got up, stiff and cold, and went out to the privy. On her way back she stood in the yard in the cool, smoky air, feeling warmth come off the bricks, listening for footsteps. Distantly she could hear the throb of machines. A train passed, going towards Birmingham, but she heard no footsteps, no one coming.

Sitting down again, she began to feel really worried. Surely Ted should have come back by now? The old Ted would have done. Fear gathered in her belly. What if he had done something terrible? The thought of the passing train chilled her. Her mind filled with images of Ted hurling himself under its wheels; of his body floating in the black waters of the cut . . . Should she go to the police? She sat back in the chair, straining her ears.

Come home. Please come home, she begged over and over again.

When the clock on the mantel struck five that Friday morning, it woke her with a horrible start. She realized that after all her tears and her worry, she must have fallen asleep. But Ted had still not come home.

Utterly drained, she set out for Joan's house. Seeing her daughter, feeding her, was a joy pierced through with pain and heartbreak.

'You all right?' Joan said. 'You look like a wrung-out dishrag.'

'I'm all right.' Grace looked down at Barbara's creamy face. She couldn't start talking now. She was too exhausted. And it was not finished. Ted had to come home, *had* to . . .

She was grateful that Joan buttoned her lip, though she could feel her sister's eyes on her. But Joan waited. The weekend, she had said. *And*, Grace thought, *I've told him. There's nothing else I can do.*

She walked back along Inkerman Street, her mind detached from the morning busyness of carts and vans and people passing back and forth. Mrs Fitzgerald's broad shape hove into view with her shopping bag and Grace avoided looking at her. All the time she was on the alert, her mind instantly analysing every figure to check if they were Ted.

Then the thought came to her, like a physical blow: I might never see him again. He might have gone – just taken off. You heard about it sometimes, men who went out to buy a packet of cigarettes and never came back. People who faded away into another life. But more chilling thoughts which had come to her in the night returned as well. Should she go to the police now? Supposing Ted had . . . Her mind would not follow this thought to the end.

Turning down the entry to the back door, she saw that the back gate was open. Before she even went into the house she could sense that someone was there. She peered in through the window.

He was sitting on a kitchen chair, his back to her. She could see smoke trailing upwards from his cigarette, almost as if it was before, in the days when things were normal. Before the war. As if nothing had happened. She stood looking at him through the window, so full of relief that he was there that for a second it felt as if everything was all right. And she was full of love for him, of tenderness, looking at the slender back of his neck. My husband, he's here. He's home . . .

But everything was not all right. Quietly, she slipped into the kitchen. He must have heard her. She stood quietly behind him, waiting.

Ted turned so that he was sitting sideways on the chair, elbow resting on the back, the Woodbine in his hand. He was not crying. Grace could not read his face as he looked at her. She looked back.

'You came back,' she said.

There was a silence. Ted looked ahead of him.

'Thank you,' she said humbly. 'I started to think maybe you . . .' She couldn't finish.

His eyes moved towards her again. After a long moment he said, 'I've been thinking.' He shook his head, as if to empty it of tormenting thoughts, and looked down. 'I can't stand . . .' It was a struggle to speak. 'Thinking about you with anyone else.'

'I don't want to be with anyone else, Ted.'

He was silent.

'It was just . . .'

'You wanted someone's arms around you. Yes – you said.' He sounded enraged again now.

'But he wasn't you,' she said. 'It was all a mistake. I wish I'd never . . .'

'But you wanted a babby. I never gave you a babby.'

In those seconds she knew that he had seen something she had not truly understood herself until now. That somewhere, deep down, she had wanted to find out whether she could have a child. Whether the lack was truly in her. And in her loneliness and all the darkness and endlessness of the war, sinfully, she had found out.

'Yes,' she whispered. 'I suppose so.'

Ted took a drag on his cigarette. She stood waiting for his judgement on her. The longer the silence went on, the more she felt sure that now she was alone. That Ted was searching for the words to separate himself from her. Her mind raced: what was she to do? The only people who could help were Joan and Norm . . .

Ted blew out a lungful of smoke. He looked at her again. 'D'you love me, Grace?'

'*Yes.*' Again she hurried over and knelt in front of him, certain. 'I love you, Ted.' She wept as she spoke. 'I never meant you any harm. I never meant . . .'

He stubbed out his cigarette and leaned forward, putting his hands on her shoulders. He seemed to her stronger suddenly, as if he had thought hard about what he was going to say.

'If you still want me, I'm your husband. I love you, girl, and I've not been much of a husband to you – 'specially not in the babby department.' He paused for a moment, bent his head back for a second before looking at her again.

'I've seen some terrible things, Grace. I don't want to talk about any of it; I don't want to think about any of it if I can help it. And this, what's happened here – it ain't the worst thing, not by a long way. It's a babby – and it ain't the babby's fault. If it's me you want and not this other fella – and I don't want to know who he was or any of the ins and outs – we can be a family. We might not've had a family otherwise and now we have. So whatever anyone else might say, why don't we make that a . . .' His voice trembled. 'A good thing – for all of us?'

Grace moved in closer to him, her streaming eyes fixed on his, hardly able to believe what she had heard or how much she loved this man for his courage, his kindness.

'Oh, Ted, d'you mean it? Would you do that?'

'For you, Gracie,' he said, wrapping his arms around her and pulling her into his bony chest, 'there's nothing much I wouldn't do.' And as she sobbed and sobbed, held by him, he said into her hair, 'So when am I going to meet this little daughter of ours, eh?'

Nineteen

This time, instead of knocking and walking straight in, she waited with Ted on the step outside Joan and Norm's house. She felt humble and full of gratitude, wanting to treat her sister with politeness. And Norm, who might be at home today, had not seen Ted since Ted had knocked him to the floor.

Joan came to the door, Davey peering out behind her. When she saw who was there, her face became very solemn.

'Oh – hello,' she said cautiously.

'Can we come in?' Grace said.

Joan stood back, giving Grace a questioning look as she passed her.

'I've told Ted,' Grace said hurriedly. They were all crowded into the narrow hall. 'And he . . .' She reached for Ted's hand. 'He wants to meet Barbara. Wants to be a father to her.'

She saw her sister's face relax. Joan looked at her brother-in-law, her face breaking into a wondering smile. Wordlessly, she enfolded Ted in her arms for a moment. Releasing him, she said, 'Come on – Her Majesty's in here.'

Ronnie and Joe, Joan and Norm's older sons, were sitting at the kitchen table and Grace said hello to them. Barbara was lying on a piece of blanket close to where Davey had evidently been playing on the floor with his toys. Grace went and scooped her up.

'Hello, darlin'',' she whispered.

Turning to Ted, tears in her eyes, she said, 'Here she is – come and meet your dada, babby.'

Ted looked nervous as Grace carried the little girl over to him.

'This is Barbara,' she told him. 'I don't really know why – I just liked it. Barbara Rose.'

Ted gazed at her. Grace could see he was moved and after a moment he reached out a finger and stroked Barbara's plump baby cheek.

'Hello, Barbara,' he said, so sweetly that Grace could not prevent the tears running down her cheeks.

Barbara took him in, seriously, with her wide blue eyes, then chortled with pleasure, bouncing in Grace's arms, and they all laughed.

'She's pleased to see yer,' Joan said, and Ted gave an uncertain smile. 'She's a lovely babby, Ted.'

Ted nodded, seeming on the verge of tears himself. 'She is.'

There was a movement at the back and they realized that Norm was standing in the doorway, unsure quite what he had walked into in his own kitchen.

'It's all right, come in, Norm,' Joan said. 'Don't stand there dithering.'

'All right, Ted, Grace,' Norm said, coming forward with a nervous smile as he took in the apparently harmonious scene in front of him.

Ted turned to him. 'Bit of a cracker, ain't 'er, our little Barbara?' he said. He went to Norm and held out his hand. 'Sorry, mate – for what happened before.'

'Oh, yer all right, Ted,' Norm said in his good-natured way. 'I should never've said what I said. Out of line, that was – sorry.'

Grace was amazed to hear Ted say, 'Seems everything's

been a bit out of line, what with the war . . . But t'aint this one's fault, is it?' He nodded towards Barbara. 'And 'er's family now, so we're all going to make the best of it.'

Ronnie and Joe were watching all this with wondering expressions.

'Oh, Ted,' Joan said, her voice full of emotion. 'I'm so glad. For both of yer.'

'So,' Grace said uncertainly, 'I think we can take her back home now?' She looked at Ted, who nodded.

'Back home where she belongs,' he said. 'With her mother and father.'

In a state of wonder and amazement, Grace walked back to Inkerman Street with her husband beside her and her little girl in her arms. Ted walked tall, seeming quietly defiant, proud almost, as if to say, *I don't care what anyone else in the world thinks about this because they don't matter a jot. This is my wife and our child. We are a family – and that's that.*

They spent all day together, in the house. Larry came round later to see about the pigeon coop, but Ted said they'd give it a miss for the day. Larry was introduced to Barbara and didn't bat an eyelid or seem to notice this was the first he had known of any baby.

'I don't think he's worked it out,' Ted said when Larry had gone. He grinned. 'Not the sharpest knife in the drawer, our Larry.'

He held Barbara and began to get to know her. When Grace breastfed her, he watched with silent awe for a few moments, then gently he said, 'Suits yer, wench. Born to be a mother, you were. You look like a Madonna doing that.'

'Oh, Ted . . .' Grace looked back at him tearfully, over-whelmed with love and gratitude.

Previously, Grace had always had Barbara in bed with her, but now her daughter was used to sleeping on her own. She made up a little bed on the floor in the back bedroom where Nora had slept, and the little girl soon settled.

Before getting into bed with Ted that night, Grace checked on Barbara. Ted came and stood in the doorway beside her.

'I never . . .' Grace started to whisper, then stopped abruptly, realizing that what she was about to say to Ted sounded like a criticism.

'I know,' he whispered back. 'You never expected to see this day – us here, with her – a family.' He sounded quite emotional. 'Nor me, wench. Nor me.'

They made love that night, before lying with their arms around each other, talking gently. It was blissful lying there together, close and warm. It felt like a miracle – the whole day had been a miracle. Grace told him something of how it had been for those of them at home, about the nights of bombing, the dark, stifling nights, and her loneliness, despite having Nora lodging with her. About the sense that it would never end, that life would just go on like this forever.

Ted said he didn't want to talk about his time in the camps – Stalag XXA then XXB, in northern Poland. But she asked again about his shoulder, and he told her it had happened on the way, when they were captured.

'I don't want to waste any more time on it than I have already,' he said. 'I want to hear about you – about how it's been here.'

When they had caught up a little on the years, she said almost shyly, laying a hand against his chest in the darkness, 'Love – tell me about your drawings. I know I

110

shouldn't have been looking. But they're beautiful. I never knew you could draw so well.'

'I never knew myself,' he said. She could feel the vibration of his voice against her hand. And she could hear that he was pleased to be asked. 'I was hopeless at school – at everything. We never had the chance, anyway. But there, it just started off as summat to do. There were these birds round the camp. Don't even know the names of most of 'em now.' He paused for a moment. 'That's summat I'll do while I'm here. Go to the library and see if I can look them up. One or two of the lads knew some of the names. Kenneth, for a start. It was just summat to get through the days at first, and then . . .'

He paused. 'If I make it back . . .'

A chill gripped her heart. 'Oh, Ted. What?'

'Well – maybe life might be different.'

'You could go to the art school,' she said. 'You're that good – like Kenneth said.'

Ted laughed. 'Art school – what, me?'

'Well, why not?'

He was quiet for a moment. 'I'd never've thought. D'you think . . . ?'

'Yes – why not give it a try?' she said. Before the war she would never have said that, she realized. It wouldn't have seemed practical. Now, it was being alive that mattered.

Ted stopped the conversation, as if he did not want to give himself hope.

'Let's just see what happens.' He kissed her cheek, and she could feel his warmth close to her in the dark. 'Enough surprises for one day.'

Grace tightened her arms around him. 'You're an amazing man, my love,' she said. 'And you really are full of surprises.'

Twenty

'We'll have to get us a pram,' Ted said as they set off that afternoon.

Grace, with Barbara in her arms, smiled up at him in wondering adoration. It was true, she had not managed to acquire anything much for Barbara except a few cast-offs of Davey's that Joan had given her and some little matinee coats she had knitted herself. Barbara's bed had been her bed and when they went out, she had simply carried her.

But Ted seemed to be embracing both Barbara and the idea that they were now a family at a speed that delighted her. She was amazed at the change in her husband over the past few days. His nights were not much better: he was still very restless, talked and sometimes shouted in his sleep. He was still as thin as a rake and hollow-eyed. But in himself he had changed.

When they were holding each other in bed last night, he had suddenly said something else that moved her to tears. She had been thanking him – again – for being so good about Barbara. She could still hardly believe how he had been about it, so kind and forgiving.

'I never expected that,' she said, holding him close. 'I thought you'd . . . Well, I don't know what I thought. That you'd throw me out, I suppose.'

'I can't say I daint think about it – just for a minute,' he admitted. 'But then I thought about my life without

112

you, Gracie, and it was the worst thing I could imagine. Even so, it's a terrible thing to say . . .' He hesitated.

She stroked his arm encouragingly. 'What, love?'

'Well, when I come back here, to Blighty, it felt as if I had nothing to, well, live for . . . Even you – I daint feel I was right for you. I was such a mess. And there was you, hanging on all this time and what comes back is me – this wreck of a husband who can't even give yer a babby. That's what I was thinking. I'd've been better off if I'd never made it back out of Germany.'

'Oh, Ted . . .' She cuddled him.

'I was a sick man then – it drags yer down in yerself. But seeing you, seeing her . . . Beautiful little thing, she is. And there's kids all over Europe, running in the streets, some of 'em – no mothers or fathers, no homes to call their own. All they need now is *someone*. And she won't know her real father, but I'll be a father to her, bless her little heart. And the best thing is, half of her's you, Gracie. And you make a beautiful mother, as if you was born to it . . . And now I've got both of yer – you and her.'

Grace was weeping quietly beside him now. The only shadow on the horizon was that Ted had to go back into the army, and a gigantic shadow it was. But in that moment, lying here under the same roof as her family, she had been completely happy.

It was a happiness she carried with her everywhere, feeling as if she was aglow with it. And now she and Ted were going for a little outing with Barbara – just round the block, to see Larry's birds.

It was a serene Sunday afternoon, warmed by the July sun, the sky a hazy eggshell blue. The three of them set off along Inkerman Street, calling a hello to some of the neighbours. Grace was so proud and happy, she didn't care who saw them now. Along the street, she caught sight of a face peering out of a front door – wide and pink in the warmth, eyes narrowed in vindictive interest. Seeing Grace staring hard back at her, she withdrew.

'Aft'noon, Mrs Fitzgerald!' Grace called to her. But Madge Fitzgerald stayed hidden in her doorway and didn't say a word. Grace could feel her eyes following them down the street. 'The old bitch'll be dying to say summat to you,' she told Ted.

'Well,' he said. 'There's nowt 'er can say 'll be any surprise to me, is there? Unless there's more you ain't telling me about, Gracie.'

'No,' she said, beaming up at him and linking her spare arm through his. 'Not a thing, Ted. No secrets.'

Larry Stubbs lived on a back yard a couple of streets away and Grace had never had reason to visit his house before. As they all went down the entry off the street, Grace could feel the cold coming off the damp walls bringing up her arms in goose pimples. The yard was half in sunlight, lighting up a pot with a red geranium in it outside one of the doors. The other half was in blue shade, and Grace could just see a tap on the wall of the yard, dripping steadily. A line of washing drooped across the middle. There were five houses on this yard, two of which backed onto the two facing the street outside, the other three at right angles to them, backing onto three houses in the neighbouring yard. Beyond the washing line, at the end was the brew house or wash house, and the shared lavatories, a whiff of which caught her nose even from this end.

'Brings it back, doesn't it?' Grace said. She had lived on just such a yard in Auntie Rose's house when they were children, and Ted had grown up on a yard as well. 'You won't have to live in one of these, Barbara,' she said. The

114

baby was taking everything in, as usual, with her big blue eyes. Ted's thin face creased into a smile.

'Not if I can help it,' he said.

'Hey – Ted!' Larry appeared suddenly out of one of the houses at the side, apparently still putting on his trousers. He hoicked them more comfortably around his waist and stood before them, grinning.

'The missus's just gone up to 'er mom's with the nippers or 'er'd've made us a cuppa. D'yer want one?'

'No, we're all right,' Ted said.

''Ello, babby!' Larry was already besotted with Barbara, although he had two girls of his own. He came up close and Barbara stuck a hand out and bitted him on the nose.

'Ow!' He pretended it hurt and reeled back. Barbara looked shocked. 'It's all right,' he said, chucking her cheek. 'You come to see my birdies, 'ave yer? Come on, then, I'll show yer.'

Ducking under a sagging pair of trousers on the line, he led them to the dusty far end of the yard, round by the ash cans. Along the blackened lavatory wall was a wooden cage, low to the ground, wired at the front.

'Here we are,' Larry said proudly. 'My lovelies, in here – my pride and joy, these are. And when 'e's ready,' Larry said to Grace, nodding his head at Ted, 'we'll be able to set 'im up with some.'

Grace's eyes met Ted's. If I ever come back, his look said, and hers burned with love and concern.

'Right – let's get my little princess out,' Larry said, squatting down. Grace could see the feathers of several birds in the coop – about half a dozen, she thought.

Larry unfastened the door of the coop and reached inside. Grace saw a gentle smile come over Ted's face. The pigeon Larry brought out was a milky chocolate brown

115

except for its white head and tail. It sat with a posing dignity in Larry's hands.

'Look, Barbara – can you see the birdie?' Grace said. The little girl stared at the pigeon with a solemn expression.

'This is a very clever lady, this bird,' Larry said to her. 'D'yer want to see what 'er can do?'

Grace would never forget this moment. Later, when Ted was back at home, when he had gone back to the army in August and within less than a week the US air force dropped first one, then another of the catastrophically damaging H-bombs on Hiroshima and Nagasaki in Japan, ending a war which had extended all around the world; after he had finished building his own coop in Inkerman Street and had his own pigeons; when he had signed up for classes in the evenings at the art school and set about changing the course of his life . . . this was the moment that seemed, looking back, to have kissed their lives with possibility.

'There you go, my lovely,' Larry said, his face turned upwards as he released his precious pigeon into the balmy air. They all watched as she spread her wings and flapped up, up into the blue, ascending like any other bird until she found her moment. She seemed to halt in the air, to flex her wings like an athlete until she flipped backwards, tipping into a roll, over and over, falling and rotating in the air until she caught herself and launched upwards again, as if drunk on space and freedom.

Grace saw her daughter's clear eyes fixed, absorbed, on the sky as the bird lifted and wheeled and tumbled and all of them gasped. And Ted clasped her hand in his and whispered in awe, 'Look at that. Beautiful. So beautiful.'

HALF PRICE OFF ANY
Annie
MURRAY
PAPERBACK IN WHSMITH

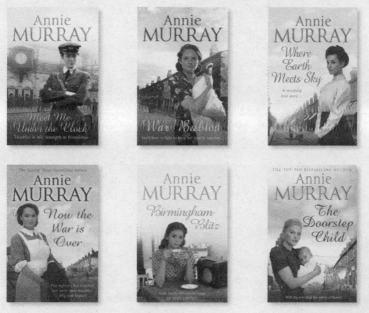

✂ -

Terms and Conditions:
This voucher is valid on one paperback copy of an Annie Murray title for only Half Price RRP £6.99 only. Valid from 01.06.17 to 31.12.17. Offer is subject to availability and is redeemable at WHSmith High Street Stores only. Excludes Outlet Stores, WHSmith Online, 'Books by WHSmith' at Selfridges, Harrods, Arnotts and Fenwicks stores, WHSmith 'Local' and all Travel Stores including those at airports, railways stations, motorway service stations, hospitals and workplaces. Offer excludes Book Customer Orders, eBooks, Kobo eReaders, and book tokens. Cannot be used in conjunction with any other multi-buy, voucher or discount card. Only one coupon can be redeemed per transaction and it must be surrendered upon use. No cash alternative available. Photocopies not accepted and coupon is not transferable. WHSmith reserves the right to reject any coupon it deems, at its sole discretion, to have been forged, defaced or otherwise tampered with.

WHSmith